good deed rain

Books by Allen Frost

Ohio Trio (Bottom Dog Press 2001)

Bowl of Water (Bottom Dog Press 2003)

Another Life (Bird Dog Publishing 2007)

Home Recordings (Bird Dog Publishing 2009)

The Mermaid Translation (Bird Dog Publishing 2010)

The Selected Correspondence of Kenneth Patchen
    edited by Allen Frost (Bottom Dog Press 2012)

The Wonderful Stupid Man (Bird Dog Publishing 2012)

Saint Lemonade (Good Deed Rain 2014)

Playground (Good Deed Rain 2014)

Roosevelt (Good Deed Rain 2015)

5 Novels (Good Deed Rain 2015)

The Sylvan Moore Show (Good Deed Rain 2015)

Town in a Cloud (Good Deed Rain 2015)

*A Flutter of Birds Passing Through Heaven: A Tribute To
    Robert Sund* edited by Allen Frost and Paul Piper
    (Good Deed Rain 2016)

At the Edge of America (Good Deed Rain 2016)

AT

the

EDGE

of

AMERICA

cause she thought he a
America really was nothing more than just time and sand
that filled an hourglass for a moment before. He watched all
things of America pile over the edge, but was most affected by
a thunderstorm with lightning of an August night he remembered
my past him. He must have
or when

At the Edge of America ©2016 Good Deed Rain

Bellingham, Washington

ISBN 978-1-945176-60-9

Writing: Allen Frost

Cover: "The Dodo" by Ruth Hulbert

Back Cover: Original self-published cover, 2004

Production Assistance: Fred Sodt

Apple by TFK!

Back in time, a 23 year old wrote this story
on a yellow notepad in NYC.
I've tried to keep this book true
to that original vision.

AT THE EDGE OF AMERICA

Bagdad Butterfly of Panama

Waterstories

Allen Frost

FOREWORD

"balloonless with the buffaloes," "what people missed, they dreamed," "the savior and his eden" – the chapter titles read as miniature poems. They evoke miniature worlds. Welcome to the vast and constantly shifting imaginary of Allen Frost. I had heard about Allen Frost before I met him, way back in 1986. My friend Neal told me that this friend of his had written a novel while in high school, called *Blue Anthem Wailing… Blue Anthem Wailing,* that title haunted me: its rhythm, which seems to build until the penultimate syllable, WAI-ling; its intrigue, which is generated by the synesthesia of the phrase - the anthem has a color; the energy of the phrase, three words that each spark individually, but that generate a *flame* when strung together. I then began to hear about the content of the book. One of the

characters was a man named "Danny" who ran the hot dog stand in the center of a small town and seemed to be a big gaseous, benevolent guy but actually wore a KKK robe beneath his hot dog vendor garb.

An America that hides its mendacity behind the face of a gladhanding fool; language and word clusters that intoxicate and even threaten to distract the reader from the narrative, but that are actually crucial incantations that cannot be separated from the multi-layered and constantly morphing worlds of the story -- as a teenager, Allen Frost was already forging key elements of his voice and vision. This voice and vision are in full flower in the two novels contained in *At the Edge of America*. A hot air balloon travels across North American geography and North American history; a man inhabits the consciousness of a dodo as this creature witnesses invasion and pillage; and we learn what could possibly be meant by the phrase, "Houdini's Arsonist Childhood." Allen Frost territory is one where the dark riddles of the "old, weird America," described by Greil Marcus in his book about Bob Dylan's *The Basement Tapes*, are allowed to roam free and where characters must find love in these haunted landscapes if they are to survive.

Dan Hanrahan
Baltimore, Maryland

INTRODUCTION

1989 was a rollercoaster, when I was a year out of school, floating between two coasts, West and East, and I landed in New York City. At that age, you're trying to find your place in the world. I already knew I wanted to be a writer. I wrote two novels in school and I was living in the publishing capital of America.

I wrote *Bagdad Butterfly of Panama* in a strange Brooklyn apartment. It was rented to my friend Rob and me by a John Lennon and Yoko Ono lookalike couple. They used to be stopped in the park for autographs, even after 1980, when people thought he was a ghost. I was inspired by the nonstop city. The writing came to me easily, but this was something new. It seems like someone's first movie, jumpy and nervous, little chapter poems like splices of film need-ing assembling. You really have to read it twice to know what's going on—fortunately you can always refer to the Chapter 60 timeline.

Two things created *BBoP* : at least once a week I would go to the American Museum of Natural History—and I used to go to an old movie theater. They only showed movies from the 1930s and 1940s, comedies and mysteries. (I'd go there right now if I could.) And over at the museum was a dodo in a glass case. As I went back and forth over the crumbling Williamsburg Bridge, rode subways to bizarre temp jobs all over Manhattan, I was putting the pieces together in my mind.

Waterstories was written hand in hand with *Bagdad Butterfly of Panama*. In late winter, I went out to Cape Cod to stay with my friend Neal, who in 23 years became the heroic seaplane pilot Jed in *Moonrise Kingdom*. It was sunny with a cold ocean wind. I returned to

NYC, staring out the window of the Greyhound. Patches of snow on the land, I saw a graveyard on the steep bank of a river. *Waterstories* came from the moment of seeing that. This book walked me right into a dark fairytale woods, mystery, danger and death. The path of this book goes even further into America's endless war, truer today than when I wrote it. And I remember the fun I had with the lines in *Waterstories*, making them move like a river. I was learning poetry.

I've been wanting to publish these two books together ever since they were written, but it's taken this long for it to happen. Looking at this writing now, I'm reminded how far away that was. A balloon and the water running in everything took me here.

Allen Frost
November 11, 2015
Bellingham, Washington

BAGDAD
BUTTERFLY
OF
PANAMA

I have no further use for America.
I wouldn't go back there if Jesus Christ
was president.

Charlie Chaplin
1953

lighter than america

plastic flowers

it was gone

leaving america in movies

balloonless
with the buffaloes

the island of mauritius
is a jewel

advice
from a caterpillar

what people missed
they dreamed

waitressing

sorry

evolution

where she had been

she had been turned
into a robot

see

the blue white house

the savior and his eden

breathing extinction
like a cigarette

getting cinematized

feathers
far as moons apart

as a butterfly in panama

6 national geographics

free from the blue
white house

the civil war

the war with japan

gone with wax

(50¢)

dreamland

the lonely parts
of the country

have befriended
the television

histories of summer

the magician's best
efforts couldn't return
the dodo

in the museum
of american history

barnstorming

1937 pancakes

peace on earth
in the days of the new
new deal

a trailer park of fire
apples

rosa parks

imaginary telephone books

he wasn't most of
the people

the people of lakehurst
talk in disaster metaphors

industrial revolutions

houdini's arsonist
childhood

rosetta stone

butterfly countdown

all was said and done
in hieroglyphics

america (strangely
enough)

with alice falling

the history of america
as remembered

alice again

1956 glass

the ruins of the land
once alive

nostalgia

at the edge of america

the moment that waterfalled

dictators and
butterflies

sunken nursery rhyme

another north dakota

mark twains

widow's walk

reamerica

Chapter 17
LIGHTER THAN AMERICA

Waking up, there was nothing but cloud so thick that he didn't know where he was. The white and the gray formed a soft wall all around him and a warm wind creaked the balloon basket. So still, quiet and far from the America he had known. He could be on foggy ground or in the tall air over mountains. In the world without the world, appearances were misleading; the things he had known to believe in, he couldn't find.

As he was wondering, the air became warmer, the wind spun the balloon uneasily and he was confronted with a large glassy eye. Out of the midst of cloudbank, it stared at him. He shouted and dropped two sandbags, but the eye rose up silently along with his balloon, clouds parting around. He and half the world were reflected in it. It closed at him and reopened. The basket of the balloon shook and he held on for his life. The eye spun from him to the right, disappearing as another huge eye appeared from the left, then that one was gone by and a giant ear stopped in front.

"I'm still not sure where I am," he said to it. He peered round the ear, looking, but there was no sign of a face or body, just the two eyes and an ear. "I...I..." he stumbled for words as the ear spun up and over, out of sight. Two nostrils soared past breathing wind. A gigantic mouth was underneath, in a smile as big as the flat ends of the world tied together with teeth.

He wanted to say something, but too quickly, the smile curled and blew his balloon down. Back in sight of the groaning metal sounds and spinning colors below, he soared toward the ground, descending faster, forced down there again.

Chapter 18
PLASTIC FLOWERS

Below him, all he saw pounded like one big factory. Shapes and colors of all sizes burst from the ground, plastic and metal and concrete, and everything had been built over shaking sand. There were no green plants and even the sky looked like a painted backdrop—which it was—the balloon crashed into its shadow on a wall of plastic blocks locked together with blue.

Gravity took over, and he went down in the crumpling balloon, dropped out of the sky, falling towards the spinning landscape. It hurt his eyes to look into the wind and he sunk low to the floor. What could he do but wait for the dream to be over? He could hear police sirens, loud voices calling, machines; he smelled the gasoline, the ring of cash registers and the sounds of war machines and all the sad crying from crowded streets. He came close enough to crash through the gray acid of pollution they pumped into their air (like it was the way they wanted to breathe), close enough for his eyes to sting.

From somewhere, close to hitting, he felt the shock—there was a police gunshot. A ricochet and a sudden wind pocket grabbed hold of him and lifted him up and out of danger. Below disappeared as an endangered species from his sight, as he was sent back up into clouds and he had been that close to returning.

Chapter 19
IT WAS GONE

It was gone. Everything disappeared quickly into darkness. The balloon took him up, out, turning slowly, creaking around. He held tightly to the twisting ropes, as if a bad dream had passed and he was slow to wake. It was such a mystery, he didn't even know if he was still living, or moving as a ghost, haunted by America and the memory of movies.

But his grip on the ropes began to weaken. There was nothing he could do. He began to slip as the cord bent and became a steering wheel in his hands and he was moved through time, driving the car to a movie theater, where he bought a ticket with hands that smelled of gasoline. And it was the butterfly that brought him here.

Most anything would happen in this

world, he was finding out. He couldn't even keep it on a map. There was no real way of controlling it all, the twists and turns. He shook his head. He realized he still had too much America in him, confusing into him. But there were windows he could go through to anywhere else, ways of being whatever he wanted to be.

He looked at the sky above the movie theater. It was dusk, some orange clouds, a few crows and a landing airplane. But that wasn't all. Three dots in formation were flying towards him. In a moment he could tell they were three Mount Rushmore-sized heads of Nixon, Reagan and Bush.

Chapter 20
LEAVING AMERICA
IN MOVIES

He started spending all the time he could in the movie theater. There was nothing else but that moving him. He didn't want to leave this wooden place. It was the only America he wanted to be in, watching the screen, watching the dreams of another world. The moment he stepped back outside, he saw the late 20th century dying to become dead. He wanted to leave that forever. In a theater that showed old black and white movies all day long, he would sit for hours. He wanted that forever.

He thought he discovered the only way. He had to leave the mobile home park burning (the reddest orange from flames eating all that tin) he had to leave his old life behind and he

came to the theater to disappear once and for
all. With a dried butterfly in his pocket and
sirens crying for him through the theater walls,
he left into the screen.

Chapter 21
BALLOONLESS WITH THE BUFFALOES

The sky's corrupt G.O.P heads exploded past him leaving a trail of fire and searing exhaust and he was plunged into a dark ocean so dark no lighthouse could find him. It was the tornado of their passing wakes that flung him out of the basket. For twenty full seconds he plummeted in the pitch black holding his arms tight around himself. He hoped there was water below him or a stack of hay a hundred feet high.

When he could see light again and breathe again, down through the clouds he saw a dark brown field. As he fell closer, he could see what covered the ground: an entire landscape of buffalo. Seconds later he crashed down amongst them. They scattered like leaves away from him.

The balloon settled down and wrapped around him. It felt like water he had to swim through.

When he emerged, he was someone else in another world.

Chapter 22
THE ISLAND
OF MAURITIUS
IS A JEWEL

The island of Mauritius is a jewel in the Atlantic. He was now a part of it. It was under his feet, wherever he walked. He was only a few feet tall and he looked down his beak, down his feathered purple chest to the claws of his feet walking the ground. All the surprise he felt came out of his mouth as a squawk. Another bird answered him, a sentence he understood.

"Nice weather today, isn't it?"

"Beautiful," he answered. He was talking about the weather like it was an egg to be rested upon thoughtfully and carefully, believing nothing else really mattered. As a dodo, he didn't even know there was more to talk about.

Out where the sun began for them every morning, where it glowed up from the water, there was a boat and then several boats floating, small black. A dodo would probably see them as water birds, spreading their wings, and the sails were rippling as they came down the masts and the big ships nested offshore.

But the birds could smell something dangerous, terrible unknowns, a storm drifting across the distance. The dodos decided to hide, all around the island they were panicked, scared, running under berry trees, hollows in rocks, wherever they could hide. What they heard was the sound of dogs barking and people shouting as the rowboats neared.

Before he could comprehend the shift in perspectives, there were new creatures crowding all over their nests and a four legged running mouth was opening up to grab him and he was chased from under leaves out onto the jagged beach.

The cries of dodo birds and feathers slowly pulled a shade over his eyes, over the sinking of a beautiful rainy day, falling water from the sky.

Chapter 23
ADVICE FROM A CATERPILLAR

What was it like to be small as a dodo then getting even smaller? It was just the world getting that much bigger. As a caterpillar, the world was images spun out forever. And everything was vibration, everything had a presence. So small, through all the directions of birds, crickets, animals, drifting pollen, all that was moving, most of all he could feel the Earth breathing. The planet breathes like a tired adding machine. Spinning itself around and around in orbit. While it turned, it all added up to him as a butterfly, with a thick green stalk under his feet. And then he was in flight.

Chapter 24
WHAT PEOPLE MISSED, THEY DREAMED

Once he tried to leave the movie theater, flushed out of the dark with visions of that film ended, and he watched the pace of the red shadow of himself on the pavement, moving faster underfoot. The roar of rocket engines rattled the buildings while he was trying to accustom his senses back to their world. Crossing the street, he glanced to his sides and there was the end of the world.

Framed between two black buildings torn into the blue sky, a white contrail was curling over. He froze as the sound went through the city with him between the lines of the crosswalk. It hung in the sky for an icy moment, a cold reflection, like a black spider dangling from a web, pausing in lowering itself down—and then the smoke curved away back up into the air. Jets screamed figure-eighting through the skyscrapers, tearing black smoke trails across the sky. He wanted to run as if the city was on fire, or soon would be.

A crowd of people on the curb were smiling, jabbing each other pointing at the performance. The streets were filled with moving flags, red white and blue tied to cars and people. Windows had flags, and ribbons were tied round trees and lampposts. Flashing low over the city, the planes shot past the windows of all the tall offices, and people stood watching, pointing and following.

Over the walls his shadow traveled, across the spraypainting and charred bricks. Escaping from the sky, he went down the cement steps underground, back to the ticket booth and paid, opened the door, back into the movie theater.

Chapter 25
WAITRESSING

She collected money from the table tops before she cleared dishes. She would put small silver coins, or dollar bills sometimes, in the pouch in her apron. She needed the money to pay for her apartment around the corner. It would be get up every day to the alarm clock, shower, get dressed and try to wake up with toast and coffee. Usually she had Saturdays off but someone would always call her if they got swamped. At five o'clock she'd awake from dreaming about dreaming. Serving plates and dishes and cups from the kitchen to tables everyday of her life, was conquering her. It made her tired all over. She knew her life wasn't supposed to be this way, but she needed the money. Sometimes, in dreaming, she wished she would be replaced by a machine, thinking, why not have robots for all workers? It could have made her bitter, like the way she closed the curtains at night and sat in the quiet.

If business was slow, she sat on a stool by the jukebox, rubbed her feet with one hand and read newspapers about Hollywood stars. These newspapers had bright photographs of people smiling their way in and out of limousines and parties. She looked up from that when he came in the door. Most of the people who came in she didn't see. They could have been shadows on the walls. She saw him and felt like she was in a movie. "Can I get you some coffee?" she was on her feet and asking with the paper falling down behind the heater. Something in her voice made a difference.

"Sure." Still fresh from the movie screen, he watched her, tried not to watch her, as she went behind the counter and came back with a coffee pot, cup and a plate with two slices of toast.

"Sure was a nice day out today," she had to say, but she was falling into his eyes too, so much that the coffee spilled over the cup rim and ran over the toast, across the table.

He was moved along the memory of that table top again until he fell off.

Chapter 26
SORRY

When he thought about what he had done to her, he was looking at himself in a reflecting pool moving with the shape of what he had become, covered with feathers. He watched the water become a blue eye to her. He saw her moving plates between tables. She moved so slowly like she was underwater until her hand stopped over a dollar on the counter. Leaves started to fall on the water surface and he could tell hours, days, seasons, had passed for her.

Chapter 27
EVOLUTION

The archaeopteryx bird was mostly a reptile with feathers. Millions of years ago it glided palm to palm like sunlight, flapping over dinosaurs. And its bones and feathers are preserved in museums like spider webs in clay. Just as long ago it seemed, where he had grown up, he used to farm the concrete in front of his house. In his hands he had a fishbowl of bugs he caught, beetles, ladybugs and potato bugs crawling about. Slender, long legged spiders made jigsaw puzzles of them-selves. They put together pictures and spelled words. When he tipped them back out, they would drift away and find their little places in the world again. Holding the fishbowl, he would watch them go. He thought about the past, how it was like holding a crystal ball that read what the future would be.

Chapter 28
WHERE SHE HAD BEEN

He was so tired, spinning corners turning him back, falling through mirrors and out again; he needed a moment of calm and he let the balloon down. The basket touched softly to the ground. He knew it would be somewhere new, he just hoped it would be welcoming.

It was a familiar world. An old red curtain was drawn across in front of him and as he watched, it opened. The thick cloth barely made a sound as it rippled, and movie light rivered overhead and she appeared, with black and white for colors. He wasn't sure where she had been hiding, like him she had been lost somewhere along in American history, but now, she was before him, stepping out of a movie.

Chapter 29
SHE HAD BEEN TURNED INTO A ROBOT

What she said was, she had been turned into a robot. "They must have programmed me to do things. It was only when I realized that, I began to change. Suddenly I had the power to change. I could be whatever I wanted." It happened a long time ago and she still couldn't hide the hope in her eyes. "For a long time I didn't know who to be." She was lost in appearances, turning into all those women of twentieth century America.

At night, next to her, he could hear static and sparkling flowers of broadcast in her ears. She was telephoning the universe. He imagined her with telescopes of beauty, going further and further out. For a moment, thinking of her, he almost caught up with her in galaxies and then—he was alone again in his balloon.

Chapter 30
SEE

A parking meter couldn't have snapped more suddenly and he was back in the basket and the sun was a bright expiring quarter going down.

Something was in his hand. He opened his fingers and there was a gold locket with a chain curled sleeping in his palm. A tiny lever opened it. In the center of the locket was a picture of her with her finest robot smile.

While he held her, she became a magnet to him. She had batteries that never tired. She could live wherever, forever long, remembering everything that happened in all her life like a moving library. He thought of her years from now, getting lost in her memories, all the corridors she had left and he hoped that somewhere in her thoughts of remembering she would reenter and find him.

He unwrapped the chain and put it around his neck like a string of digital daisy-chain. He wondered what this meant, why all that remained of her was a picture. The gold was smooth and he rubbed it with his thumb.

Suddenly he heard her voice, talking from the photo, "See," she smiled. Her voice signaled to him from miles, bright as the invention of shortwave radio, following the soft contours of land, "I'm still with you."

Chapter 31
THE BLUE WHITE HOUSE

A spark passed through her talking image and shocked him with a blue miniature of lightning. "Ouch!" She was always doing that to him. Maybe she thought that was love. There was no use explaining love to a robot. He had tried and ever since then, she'd been taking it out on his nervous system.

The blue White House palace was down below and he piloted for the marble courtyard. It had been built by a billionaire here in the middle of cornfields.

He soared down for a bumpy landing on the shiny blue courtyard. The water in the fountain was also blue.

The robot woman pictured around his neck spoke up but only had this to say, "It all looks so beautiful, doesn't it?"

It was something he remembered and his response by stepping out of the basket was turning into a dodo again. He couldn't help himself. It was just as the billionaire owner appeared, in a carriage drawn by a flock of passenger pigeons.

Chapter 32
THE SAVIOR AND
HIS EDEN

The passenger pigeons stopped beating the wind and settled down on the marble like 19th century newspapers. He stepped out of the carriage's glass door and scattered bread-crumbs before him.

The birds had been waiting for that and were quick to eat. A panda bear made a mad dash across the courtyard and seconds later a whooping crane came hopping after. The billionaire stepped across the space of blue marble towards the dodo. "Welcome to my land, Dodo."

His nervous beak clattered with diner dishes of porcelain. To ensure himself that it was happening, he tried to say something about the weather. The words failed. He tried to close his eyes on it, but his big eyes blinked their dodo vision and came back to where they had left off.

"You're lucky to be here, and I'm lucky to have found you," the man said. From behind his back came a net.

But to a dodo, the net looked like a thick spider web, or something scratched into the sand of sweet Mauritius where there were no natural enemies, no men and no nets and dodos could live in total happiness.

The net was stinging tight around his feathers and he was crying out in fear.

Chapter 33
BREATHING EXTINCTION
LIKE A CIGARETTE

The voice came from above him and said, "Don't be afraid." The passenger pigeons were reigned back airborne. It was tight quarters inside the sliding along carriage, even tighter for the dodo wrapped up in the net. Corn swished all around them, parting with the sound of a rowboat sighing over weeds.

"You're very lucky to have come to me," he continued, pressing numbered buttons on the wall. They started to move to the left. There were numbers blinking above the door. Number 201 just flashed and then 202 and on they went. "I save animals from extinction. I bring them here. I'm a collector of endangered lives. It's my job to collect those that need protection. They all come to me eventually. There's a perfect place for you here and you'll never have any fears. You'll live in perfect happiness here."

The carriage slowed.

"Here we are."

The passenger pigeons had landed. The net came off him and he leaped outside into the yellowing stalks of tall corn.

"You're the only dodo I've got. I'm so pleased and so surprised with my luck!" A Hemingway big game hunter smile saluted his catch and he winged his passenger pigeons into the sky to pull him onwards, waving out the door a goodbye. "You'll like it here!" His last words vanished like Bengal tigers through the green stalks.

Chapter 34
GETTING CINEMATIZED

She spoke to him through the gold picture around his feathers. Her voice was not like a robot, but more than human, it was 1000 Hollywood women in robes smiling and the light was perfect on them, *Casablanca* black and white softly. Already, he could feel changing. She said to him with cinemascope beauty, "Don't worry, I'll get you out."

Chapter 35
FEATHERS FAR AS MOONS APART

And then, like a squeeze, she gave him a reassuring shock. A little of his purple feathers burned up past his beak, smoke signals. All he had to do was think of her. He thought about her until he suddenly realized the darkness all around him and the moon being swum in the cornstalks swaying. He felt sad, alone like the last dodo alive and dodos weren't supposed to feel things like that and so he was changing slowly back into a human. Human feelings flowed into him. Once again there was tingling in his toes and fingers. He decided to walk.

The grass snapped around him. The plants had been woven into an iron curtain wall, in front of him and around him, penning him in. But he found he could climb over it now. As he did, it swayed gently under his heavier weight. Sitting straddled on the top of the fence, he was ten feet tall and could take a look around himself.

Corn was everywhere; ocean liners would have been lost in it all. There was no way out.

A mastodon put its trunk up to his leg. He patted its fur and it purred. He was surprised to know that mastodons purred, but he was more startled to see all the animals poured like Noah's ark in all directions penned around him.

A compass of animals and the sounds of a zoo independence day as they greeted him, their voices passing from growls, barks, tweets, shrieks, and hisses filling the horizons with sound. The sound they all made together stretched like a rainbow. They had never heard of anyone getting out of a cage before. Not even birds could fly out. Something had held them all in. They'd all been trapped since arriving. But it had been designed to keep animals in, not people.

Chapter 36
AS A BUTTERFLY
IN PANAMA

There was a butterfly on the inside of the wall next to him, down below him, set in the leaves like some flower. (As a butterfly in Panama, it had lived before the digging of the canal to connect oceans and continents. So softly, it needed the mud and green trees and blue air. They became extinct when the empire digging machines bit apart its nests. But here it lived with no sand, buckets or shovels in sight…Safe.)

"Lower me to him," said the robot of 1000 movie screens. Holding the necklace by the chain, he did. The gold twinkling attracted the butterfly to pad over and step onto its shine. He pulled it back up slowly. The orange wings flickered. "Careful," she said. "Make sure he stays when you put the necklace on."

He slowly put the chain over his head. The butterfly remained.

She said, "Turn the necklace around so it rests on your back."

"Okay."

When it was, he felt the wings start to grow. Oranging out of the locket, they expanded like petals until he looked like a gigantic Bagdad Butterfly of Panama. The wings beat the air, lifted him up, and began to fly him away.

Chapter 37
6 NATIONAL GEOGRAPHICS

She warned him, "You ought to let the butterfly know that you're headed for the moon." It was true, the moon was getting closer and the butterfly was determined to get there.

He asked the butterfly wings, "Why don't we go to the ground instead of the moon."

The wings listened and took him down slow and spiraling as any Bagdad flying carpet. The air whistled past.

...There is a fine preserved specimen of the Bagdad Butterfly of Panama. It is pinned all alone in a teak display box underneath half a set of 1937 *National Geographics* and an unsealed envelope of supermarket coupons from sometime in Summer 1963, deep in the mysterious catacombs of the American

Museum of History. Its orange wings are still bright like a Battle of Midway pilot in his raft shouting, waving to a boat on the horizon. Its eyes were mummified, peeled from rocks in the Euphrates. Dead, it is just a hieroglyphic of a butterfly...

The Bagdad Butterfly of Panama wings landed him safely on the ground. They deflated back into the locket and he could see where he stood, in the courtyard of the Blue White House.

Chapter 38
FREE FROM THE BLUE WHITE HOUSE

He could also see the balloon. It was a bright red tomato. He started to run towards it.

Around him the air and ground shook with the heavy approach of a stampede.

He dived into the gondola, cut the holding ropes and became part of the sky again. The blue palace White House was lost in a growing storm. When he escaped, so did all the other animals.

He disappeared into clouds.

Chapter 39
THE CIVIL WAR

And for some reason, the clouds reminded him of the suds in the sink, back home in a green lit neighborhood of mobile homes not far from the municipal airport. The nights were filled with the sounds of the interstate and crickets. Inside, dishes with blue decorative trim soaked under soapsuds, waiting like clean shark fins. His wife was furious, wanting to know why he quit his job at the factory. Did he really think he could spend all his time at the movies? Things had fallen apart between them. The love had fallen between the cracks.

Another voice was coming through. Far away, she was calling him from the necklace.

A mobile home was burning to the ground in a small town next to an airport in North Dakota. He spun back to the man standing there with a gas can and matches and his work was done.

He blinked away from him, her and them and everyone and everything there.

Chapter 40
THE WAR WITH JAPAN

Like a pilot shot down, he was alone with words to himself on the water. Underneath him were fathoms of sunken warships and crews. He had been stranded for days in a small orange raft in the middle of blue waves, nights and days of revolving sky. The United States chose its wars and for some reason, unreal as a dream, he had been bombing the people below. His airplane soared above them like death until it crashed him in the sea. He was miles from land and further still from home. When a Bagdad Butterfly of Panama blended in with the gold of his inflatable raft, he stretched a slow hand towards it. It took off in the direction of an approaching minesweeper.

Chapter 41
GONE WITH WAX

They went to Niagara Falls, that thundering natural wonder on the border of America, with more wax museums than any other bumper sticker attraction. She was angry that he was so fascinated by the wax museums. She told him she was beginning to think he came here for the wax likeness of Neil Armstrong, Marilyn Monroe or Elvis Presley rather than for her and their honeymoon. There was still rice in his hair as he stared at Scarlett O'Hara. She was part of the wax museum's tribute to Hollywood.

Chapter 42
(50¢)

She bought a 50¢ bumpersticker souvenir for their new car. He had a postcard of a wax President Kennedy.

Chapter 43
DREAMLAND

He returned to her Caribbean glowing eyes and her smile with Bagdad Butterflies of Panama kindness. She had the kind of patience only a robot could have. She knew she was in love with a time machine and that sooner or later he would find the right place to be with her. She was waiting for him to say something to her, wearing the dress from a popular magazine of 1952.

The way she could still love America, he just couldn't understand. It seemed to be her only weakness as a robot, that she could accept America as a beautiful dream. He never told her what it was really like to live there and how it had failed. He didn't want to tell her that America had failed and even worse; he liked her smile for it all. It was part of her love.

She said she had been programmed as a waitress. He knew something about waitresses too—his wife was a waitress. The way her eyes would thrill to look at him, as if she would never tire of him. She had met him by pouring coffee on his toast by accident. Apologizing with paper napkins, she offered to take him to a movie and of course he accepted.

Later on, that night of the fire, his wife was wearing a nurse's uniform. It was Halloween at the diner. The cook was wearing a rubber nose with mustache and thick eyebrow glasses attached, overacting back and forth with dishes like *The Marx Brothers in a Night at the Kitchen*. She could see an orange glow through the window. All she could say was, "Oh my God!"

Chapter 44
THE LONELY PARTS OF
THE COUNTRY

He floated over, in the balloon the color of tomato season. She was gone, disappeared love with static long minutes ago. He was alone in the sky with the land below mirroring his loneliness. A scratchy Cisco Houston record was the spinning land and the clouds played their shadows across, down on those below, on the homeless nation. The balloon descended the way of cloud shadows.

And as the balloon got closer to the ground, he saw boxes grazing in the gray field he would be landing in shortly. Gray blue static was playing on their screens. Abraham Lincoln could have given the Emancipation Proclamation across to those cold faces.

He landed in a Gettysburg of TVs.

Chapter 45
HAVE BEFRIENDED
THE TELEVISION

He saw a strange America in the TV screens, as he watched them shimmering, electricity. Like the poison of the Bagdad Butterfly of Panama that he ate that night at the movie theater, there was a moment of perfect stillness and then everything changed.

Chapter 46
HISTORIES OF SUMMER

Like peeling paint and wasps building under the eaves, Summer came to his understanding and he leaped out of the basket and ran to the nearest TV. He turned the set off and immediately he was merged in a fairground, like a tintype of Coney Island.

With birds singing in the warm wind—it must be summer, maybe late July—he set forth, wearing a pin of the Bagdad Butterfly of Panama on his coat lapel. It shined like the insignia of a lost army of New World conquistadors, covered over in butterflies, laid into the mud of what will be a canal someday, and more conquistadors sinking, histories ahead in the future.

There were rides, a Ferris Wheel and a

Rollercoaster and a Flight To Mars, covered with lights, moving across and all over the ground. Walking on sand, it was all sliding into evening, the sun going out softly as the gaslight of a stove. Glowing on the ocean, the jigsaw puzzle of daylight shimmered on water. The happiness of the moment turned him into a dodo, and he helped himself to a beak full of cotton candy offered by a pinstripe circus ringmaster and a fire-eater grinned.

Chapter 47
THE MAGICIAN'S BEST EFFORTS COULDN'T RETURN THE DODO

The glass case was something he could see through, but trapped him. He had been in it for months touring the countryside as *The Last Living Dodo!* He hadn't mentioned the weather in months. In fact he had not said anything at all, not a squawk. The Last Living Dodo was dying. He looked at his still reflection in the light of his glass case. He wasn't the same. People began to look at him sadly; twenty five cents of sadness was what they paid for.

The magician with the rabbits in his coat tried his best to make the dodo look happy again. He put powder in the feathers, shined the beak with a shoeshiner's skill and sprayed perfume on the rumpled tail.

The trapeze artist watched her perfume going to waste on a dodo, "Not too much!" she cautioned the magician. It was her only bottle.

"This isn't too much," he sprayed and coughed.

"That's way too much!" she yelled and stomped over to him and took her crystal bottle back. "Look how much you wasted! Didn't do a bit of good! Look at him!"

The dodo was fast becoming a doorknob with feathers, dying.

"Well, I tried." The magician closed the dodo's door. "I tried my best." He went outside the trailer and had a smoke. Not much else could be done.

When the bird died, the circus sold the body to a museum for $50. The ringmaster bought a ring with the money and proposed to the trapeze artist. She agreed and two months later they quit the circus and moved to California.

Chapter 48
IN THE MUSEUM OF AMERICAN HISTORY

The Museum of American History stuffed him and mounted him in a glass case labeled *The Last Living Dodo*. He was a posthumous bird statue record. But there was still something of himself alive in that…Inside the dodo he waited imprisoned for the chance to get out somehow.

He waited nearly a year. Time moved so slowly inside a stuffed bird. He had a lot of time to think about Mauritius weather and what the dodos were all about. Nobody else thought so much about dodos as he did—it was the national bird of his thoughts. People stopped to look at him for a while, then moved on to the pelicans and owls.

One evening, cold in the glass, he had

a dream about her, finally remembering, and in the morning she was there. As he slowly opened his eyes, she was waiting, wearing a blue kimono with rare birds pictured all across the silk.

She stood in front of him and promised out of breath, "I came here as soon as I could!" Her hands touching to the glass, he stood up out of the case and reached for her, standing out of broken glass and feathers.

Chapter 49
BARNSTORMING

"It's not easy being as a dodo, believe me," he told her as they floated over 1930's American farmland. "When you're used to having no fears and knowing no dangers, then out of the blue, meeting that kind of world is destructing."

"Yes, but nobody should like the weather that much," she laughed, closer.

Later with the moon, he looked down on 1930's small town America and there were still forests, small towns, and he thought of movie theaters down there. Sleeping trees below, they descended slowly into a clearing, a moonlit field, sighing down like a nesting owl.

She was a silhouette standing next to him. "This is where you wanted to be," she said. "This is that America." Then she wasn't even a shadow.

She was gone when he woke up.

A brown sedan was parked next to him and it sounded its horn, abruptly shattering his visions of her with the golden years of big band.

Chapter 50
1937 PANCAKES

"Say, that's quite a balloon, mister!" he heard called out and the words rang up to him in the tree branches. He looked over the edge of the basket.

She took him to a time devoted to 1937. The people here lived 1937; 1937 forever skipping like a record.

A brand new sedan was parked not more than twenty feet from him and a man put on his hat as he got outside to see the balloonist. The 1937 man stood there waiting for the balloon to do something, but it was frozen like a factory of hot air.

He dropped out of the balloon basket, "Morning!" and walked over.

In less than ten minutes they were eating a diner breakfast for only quarters and dimes.

And it tasted so good! The 1937 pancakes were served with real sweet maple syrup and fresh eggs.

There was something familiar, he knew, about the waitress who brought the food. She was wearing a disguise. Waitresses and mysteries and America, that was her game, and she poured his coffee perfectly. Her eyes, sparking with blue, were anticipating radars; she was flirting like an electric toaster.

He pretended not to notice it was her and "Thank you," is what he said to his perfectly poured out coffee.

He noticed her lips start to pout and then smile, "Would you like cream with that, sir?" She was starting to glow again. She knew he would.

"Sure," he pushed his cup over to her and she poured the white in.

"Would you like anything else, sirs?"

He smiled at the F.D.R pin on her blouse.

She was really trying to fit in with 1937. She waited, warm currents were in her, watching him for entertainment (before the television had come to America) waiting for him to say something. She held the coffee pot steam like the torch of the Free World.

"I'd like some orange juice please," the man with the brand new car replied. "And those pancakes were so good, I'd sure like some more." Before Europe was collapsing into war again and again over there, all he wanted was orange juice and pancakes.

"Of course," her smile moved to that man and became the standard waitress manual smile.

He said, "I'll have some more pancakes too," and her smile reappeared on the electric peach of her face. He wanted to get up and say he knew it was her, but he was enjoying her game. She wanted so badly to give him a shock, but she knew she shouldn't. The tension turned her hair orange, but nobody seemed to notice.

Rita Hayworth in her hair, she went to the kitchen door and called in "Two more orders of pancakes."

Chapter 51
PEACE ON EARTH
IN THE DAYS OF
THE NEW NEW DEAL

They left the diner with an exact duplicate of a 1937 day shining its sun.

He had leaped back to the radio vacuum tube days of 1937. He thought it would be better for everyone...This new 1937 rolling back. The return to the past was an experiment to stop the endless wars to come. It was the only hope for America, to go back to what was the past and correct with hindsight. There would be no more mistakes, and no battleships in 1941 Pearl Harbor. Instead, Pearl Harbor was building the largest drive-in theater in the world with a movie screen that would face the ocean where the warm Pacific would crowd to see the release of *Lost Horizon*.

He had a feeling she'd be one step ahead of him; the next waitress at the next diner. Somewhere, she was moving things along perfectly and the atom bomb would never be invented.

Chapter 52
A TRAILER PARK OF FIRE APPLES

But she was more clever than he anticipated. He should have remembered how much she loved mysteries and how she had memorized Agatha Christie. She could fit herself into any mystery. She was waiting when he decided to go see a film, drink one in like a cider, as the brown evening began to cool.

And there she was in the ticket booth; flower papered inside like a dahlia calculator. She was wearing a red uniform. When she passed him his ticket, she couldn't help giving him a shock. She couldn't help herself; she didn't know what would happen. It sent him spinning like a comet out of 1937's orbit and he returned to a North Dakota night of burning.

There was a blue matchbox in his shirt pocket which held the crumpling papyrus of an orange butterfly. A picture on the back of the matchbox was an appeal to start stamp collecting with this special offer.

He was running from his mobile home after splashing gasoline on the aluminum walls and porch and tossing the can on the roof. He went through both cans of gas and nobody noticed him doing it—it was late and he was the Johnny Appleseed of gasoline, planting orchards to bloom in the trailer park. He watched the crop bear fruit by lighting a match. Standing in the driveway, he bent down and cupped a hand round a lit match. And he dropped the flame to the gas. The fire galloped away from him and hit his house. Even the pumpkin on the porch was on fire.

And he turned away slowly with the turning of his last page and left for the movies. It wasn't far. People were trying to shout out the fire behind his back. And this was finally the last act, ridding himself of the last obstacle in his path because he knew his wife was already gone. She paid him no more attention than a fly's shadow.

When he was in the theater, he was passing into a new life. He knew he wouldn't come back to the same world. A Bagdad Butterfly of Panama was in his pocket. He could feel the shape of the matchbox. He could hear the sirens through the theater like thunder outside the walls of movies.

While the man sitting three seats behind him was eating popcorn, he had a butterfly. His last sight was Ginger Rogers and Fred Astaire. They were dancing in the biggest hotel room he had ever seen, white as clouds, with ceilings that were skies, and wings began to carry him up.

Chapter 53
ROSA PARKS

Something was wrong with this 1937 though. He saw it in the balcony above him and the backs of buses and in people's houses and jobs and schools, where people could eat or drink or sleep, and written on doors where people could go. He could see it in people's eyes and the way they moved. It was painted on everything. As he experienced this time, he felt some of the people weren't created as equal as other people and his dream was collapsing and falling apart the more he noticed, the more he thought about it. He tried to concentrate on the film and forget 1937. But it was getting harder and harder to accept the film when he could see through it.

Chapter 54
IMAGINARY TELEPHONE BOOKS

When he came out of the theater, the evening had settled in to sleeping and there were pink clouds moving very quietly in the stars. He could look at the sky instead of 1937, but she was waiting for him on the street corner. She had a dark green overcoat and a hat with feathers and she was humming Count Basie as she walked towards him in the moths of streetlamps.

A sweep of her brown hair froze in the corner of her lips when she said, "Hello." Her pretty eyes caught the yellow light of closed store windows glowing from across the street.

He said, "You know, you look very familiar."

She pushed the hair away with a blow

and blinked once like a very far away familiar mirage. "I should…" She was moving her foot sideways as if she had mastered ballet and could dance on the moon if she wanted.

The moon would never again be walked on by astronauts. Whole histories wouldn't happen as America would revolve round 1937, maybe drifting a little forward or backwards, like a cheap watch keeping time.

"I just can't place it…" He pretended to thumb through pages of names in the air, imaginary telephone books to recall.

She put her hand on her hip and was about to say something when he laughed and took her hand and saw that her bright eyes were returning again, sparkling with goldfish. And even though she was a robot, she had all the gentleness of Arbor Day calendared in her. She planted fifty trees somewhere nearby just by smiling like that.

But it didn't last long. He lost her

somewhere in the cover of shrubs and a blooming dogwood tree.

Chapter 55
HE WASN'T MOST OF THE PEOPLE

The way out was a balloon, but not his balloon. It was time for the 1937 burning of the Hindenburg. Most of the people were actually thrilled to be flying, sipping the champagne and looking at the farmland below. He knew what would soon be happening, he was doing everything he could to find her. It was his turn to save her.

It was a big airship and she could be anywhere. His locket was only a smiling photograph of her and he couldn't reach her through it. As he hurried, he talked to her over and over with no reply. He thought for sure she would be on board, maybe even flying the ship, but she wasn't anywhere to be seen among the uniforms. He showed everyone he met the locket picture of her in hopes that someone would recognize her. No one did.

A shadow crept hugely across New Jersey.

"She must have a plan...A plan for what?" He didn't know what she was up to, he wasn't even exactly sure about the fate of the voyage, if they really would all crash. Did they have to? He went to a window to try to relax and watch for her.

New Jersey was rolling out the red carpet below.

Chapter 56
THE PEOPLE OF LAKEHURST TALK IN DISASTER METAPHORS

How did a calendar work that kept repeating itself over and over? People got used to it. People convinced themselves that the year would always be 1937 until they learned to be better people. Otherwise they were just headed for destruction. Meanwhile, floating closer, so was the Hindenburg.

Lakehurst, New Jersey was writing its name with history and zeppelins. And he and the Hindenburg and all the passengers and crew were in for more than they bargained for in terms of fire. Just as the shadow was about to turn into light, his necklace alerted him, "Get ready to jump, I'm right below you."

"Jump?" He leaned against the window

and searched the field below, where a woman wearing a yellow dress waved a white parasol at him. "Jump?!" he called to her again, but he didn't get to say anymore. Caught in the sudden explosion, his lungs were filled with hot. Orange flame shot back and forth.

He was thrown from the zeppelin, he was in the air, falling and into his spinning vision The Three Republicans of the Apocalypse returned. Screaming into the smoke and fire, they crashed through the disaster and before he could yell out for help or notice what she was doing below, he landed in the soot and charcoal hair of the demon Ronald Reagan. Charging in dagger formation, they carried him away from 1937.

Chapter 57
INDUSTRIAL REVOLUTIONS

On the coal spewing head it was like the moon landing. He crossed through a vacuum of silent darkness, a lunar park honoring the small footsteps of Neil Armstrong. Everything was quiet upon the head of the 40th president of USA—he remembered the night of that election, when he threw a shoe through the TV screen in protest—and all around was filled with black swirling smoke.

Chapter 58
HOUDINI'S ARSONIST CHILDHOOD

He was dropped back where he thought he left for good. There were flashlights in the aisles of the movie theater. Why was he back? Had the butterfly returned him? Did its poison fail him? Credits on the screen were rolling, music was playing. He was lying down in the space between seats on popcorn and the stick of coca cola on the floor. He was hiding from those flashlights. When the houselights went on, he knew he would be caught. His hands smelled of gasoline. He took a chance and crept out, panthering among the people leaving.

A policeman at the door grabbed him and pulled him up, shouting, "I got him, over here!" The policeman shook him, reached for his handcuffs, and there were visions in his crocodile eyes of jail with its bars on windows and doors. This was the end.

It happened so fast, he was running before he knew just what he had done, how he got away with a Houdini of strategy.

"Freeze!" and there were screams like a disaster movie, people scattering, dropping to the cement as the uniformed man with crocodiles for reasoning pulled out his issued gun and aimed at the running arsonist.

She was holding him like lightning bugs in a jar as he awakened slowly for her. She shook him back.

Chapter 59
ROSETTA STONE

The creaking noise was the balloon basket being swayed by the moon. Wind in the clouds was warm enough so that he was not cold. She was sitting next to him and her words came from far away, a gramophone singing to wake him up.

When he tried to sit up, the record skipped and, "No," she purred, "Don't try to sit up. You fell all the way from a zeppelin. It's a good thing I was there to catch you."

She twirled at her dark hair. There were encyclopedias to unravel. Sometimes she wondered if he didn't speak a whole different language than her. She was colored by the light of the Moon and it wasn't easy for her to say she had been wrong. "So what did you think of your 1937?"

"I was wrong, it wasn't mine. It definitely wasn't where I thought I could belong." But he didn't want to say anymore. He didn't want to have to say, "I just wanted to live in a movie. That's the way I wanted life to be. I didn't want all that reality." He didn't want to ruin her beautiful ideas; he knew she was dreaming too.

"Yes, I had a feeling we may have outlived our 1937 welcome." She pointed to the Big Dipper's cupful of stars. "So here we are again." She knew how he had given up on America. There wasn't the faintest sign of presidents anywhere.

Chapter 60
BUTTERFLY
COUNTDOWN

10)   His wife left at 2:50 to the diner for the 3:00-11:00 shift. She left the insults and her arguments jackknifed to the wall like portraits of assassins. She would have two cups of coffee before working, telling the cook what an idiot she was married to. She was wearing a nurse's dress and a stethoscope necklace.

It was Halloween.

9)   She had left the dishes sitting in soap since her 2:50 PM departure. She told him to rinse them, "If you can do anything that requires that much intelligence!" He forgot about the dishes and they burned along with the rest of the mobile home later that evening, curling to brown in the steaming water, like melted manta rays.

8) He watched through the kitchen window as she left for the diner.

She was so mad she kicked the mailbox post and broke a heel off her shoe. She threw the shoe at the cold garden and weeds.

She walked the rest of the way hobbling like a farewell to a World War I Hemingway nurse. Her pair of tennis shoes for waitressing were under the counter at the diner. He watched her white sock as she turned the oak tree corner.

7) The shoe in the garden was the only thing of hers that survived the fire. Her parents' wedding photo—from 1939 Poland—became ashes. She didn't even bother to pick up the heelless shoe the next morning.

6) After she was gone, he felt that she was gone finally for the last time. Really gone, she had left him forever, and there was no use living with the memories she left behind. Like light bulbs there was no more light in them.

5)   So he drove to the hardware store, the gas station and the grocery store for supplies. The hardware store was a red brick building with two large glass windows that looked into rows and walls covered with all sizes and shapes of objects. He opened the front door and the string of brass bells rang as the door swung and shut behind him. He found four gas cans against the back wall and took them to the register to pay.

That was all he needed. Then he took them to the gas station and had them filled with Regular. They sat in the back seat waiting while he went into the grocery store to get candy and matches. He put the grocery bag in the back seat with the gas cans and felt very satisfied with the way they looked. His life was completing itself very nicely.

4)   When he got home, he went straight inside. There was an old movie that started ten minutes ago, the last one he would watch in

there.

Then he decided he better get that matchbox from his sock drawer before he forgot. The blue matchbox was between a pair of gray and white socks. He put it in his shirt pocket. It contained a butterfly. He watched the movie on TV.

3) With the dark came trick or treaters. At first he was startled by the goblins on the doorstep, and then he remembered the candy in the bag. He gave them chocolates and they went away.

More trick or treaters kept showing up throughout the evening, off and on. At 10:15 he decided to put his plan into action.

2) He poured four cans of gas in and on his house. He poured gas in the hallway, on the bed and the dining room table. He even climbed on the roof like a mobile home gardener watering its flat aluminum. He poured some gas down the chimney and nearly slipped getting back down. He poured a gasoline path from his house to the road and imagined himself a cliffhanger villain gunpowdering a trapped hero's cabin as he lit a match and dropped it to the ground.

1)	It worked like a charm. He watched the house burn for a moment, with neighbor's ringing the flames and kids eating their candy from paper bags. Then he got in his car and drove to the movie theater. Police cars and fire trucks passed him in the opposite lane. There weren't many people in the theater and the film was almost over. All he needed was that black and white reassurance.

0)	He took the matchbox out of his pocket and poured a dust of dried butterfly onto his tongue and swallowed. The butterfly was highly toxic and he was tired of the terrible world. It didn't take long. The jungles of Panama took him by the hand.

Chapter 61
ALL WAS SAID
AND DONE IN
HIEROGLYPHICS

He asked her once how she could have faith in hope for America when Chief Joseph, Sitting Bull, Harriet Tubman, Martin Luther King Jr., Malcolm X and so many more on through the years, all met what was evil and lost.

She said they were what held America from disappearing. She said they circled around a dream which existed because of them. It was supposed to be something beautiful, a dream that had no need for poverty, racism, prejudice, discrimination, or pain. To her, America was something to be fulfilled. It was waiting to be seen.

He didn't want to say it wouldn't

happen, he didn't want to tell her what it was like to live there. Maybe a robot didn't know what it was like to live. It was so hard to understand, not something that could be programmed.

"What did you think of me when you first saw me?" he asked her. She had her brown arms around him. She could have crushed the Titanic into a tin can with those same soft arms, but with him they were love, and flowers that grew on Venus may have been that glow in her eyes.

She smiled as she remembered him wearing the white captain's suit on the deck of the ship, steering it into harbor, the boat a gleaming of black Persian metal. His entrance was as perfect as any Bogart movie could be.

She was on the dock, dreaming of such moments—robots dream too. Her hair down to her ankles was blowing as orange as the fire he'd just come from. She was waiting for the right ship, like a lighthouse.

The boat slid to the dock, tied up with the throwing of lines ashore and the scramble of deckhands to knot the big boat down. Then he came down onto the pier. All was said and done in hieroglyphics between them. She could have moved pyramids with the way she was. How could a robot feel all this?

The balloon was flying over an ocean where whales surfaced and spouted with no fear, blue whales moved their hundreds of feet silently below them without a sound.

"You know what?" he said.

"Hmmm?" she squeezed his arm ever so slightly; she could have been holding a rabbit.

"I felt exactly the same way."

Chapter 62
AMERICA
(STRANGELY
ENOUGH)

They remembered their Panama meeting as they slowly descended...how he sold the boat and bought the balloon, how they married somewhere over Costa Rica, sailing on their way North from Central America. Jungles underneath them, thick green, with no intentions of bulldozers and chainsaws. (He had found himself in a world where it was understood such beautiful things could not be destroyed.)

The balloon landed. He rolled out asleep as it rose again, into the night with the moon controlling pulleys to the puppet of balloon. The wind was carrying it away from him. He slept on the asphalt as if it was a bed and didn't wake up until morning.

He knew he was in America (strangely enough) and he knew it wouldn't last. He waited for the cement and tar to change, for the ground to become what wasn't and then he was sliding, falling down, down and deeper down and into darkness. Into the kind of down that seems to have no end.

Chapter 63
WITH ALICE
FALLING

After a while, he was no longer afraid of falling, he even slept. He didn't know for how long. It was so black he saw unreal things projected—he saw Alice falling next to him. She was chasing after a white rabbit, and they talked for a time as they both shared the fall. She was very polite and when a kettle appeared beside them, she offered him tea. But when she was gone, off on her adventures, he was still going down.

Light was finally brought by a sofa. He floated over to it and sat down. It was a very soft sofa that glowed plaid. He reached over to the dim shape of a lamp beside him and felt for a switch to turn it on, running fingers around it until under the shade he found a cord.

When he pulled it, the light switched on and he could see everything around him. He sat on the sofa in a small round room, with a pharaoh on a throne across from him.

Chapter 64
THE HISTORY
OF AMERICA
AS REMEMBERED

"It's been a long time since I had any visitors," the pharaoh said. He had been away from the African sun for a long time. Like a prisoner he had long since covered the walls with hieroglyphics and bright tomb painting, over and over again. His voice croaked, "The last person to visit me told me that Africa had been carved up and controlled by invaders. I laughed, I said that's impossible! And she said that many of us were taken away from Africa, across the ocean to slave away and make the New World. I told her again that was impossible! It troubles me though, because she swore it was true..."

"Well..." he answered the pharaoh,

"I don't know much about history. I'm still learning it. I worked at a factory. I watched movies." He stared at the colored walls. "I guess it's true though. I'm from that New World. It's called America."

"America."

"Yes." He wished there was some way the pharaoh could picture it. He searched his pockets and found a dollar which he passed over. "Look..."

The pharaoh examined the papery green and gray in his hand.

"That's George Washington on that side. We pay respect to our leaders by putting them on money. He was our first leader. On the other side is..."

"Ahah!" The pharaoh pointed to the picture on it, "A pyramid! And the eye of Osiris! I know these!" The pharaoh was very pleased.

"Yes, well..."

"Do you build pyramids too?"

"Not exactly, no we don't. Well, maybe. We build a lot of skyscrapers."

"These words…What do they say?" The pharaoh passed the dollar back for him to read.

"Ummm…I'm not sure, it's ah Latin, I think. We don't speak this language. I'm not sure why it's there actually. But this underneath says 'The Great Seal' and then over here under the eagle 'Of the United States.' That's the United States of America." He passed the note back to the pharaoh to see. "The eagle is our symbol. The olive branches and arrows mean peace and war."

"Yes, I know this bird. But this is all very strange to me…" He flipped the paper over again and looked at Washington. "Did this man come to my Africa? Did he meet with our great kings?"

"Actually…I don't know too much about him. I know he had wooden teeth. He never lied. He once chopped down his father's cherry tree then admitted he did it."

The pharaoh looked confused.

"He was the general in the fight for our country's independence. He crossed a river of ice and starved at Valley Forge. Then he won independence for America and became our first president..."

"Yes, but what about the Africans?"

"I don't know. I think he owned slaves. I'm pretty sure." He remembered, didn't the Pharaohs use slaves to make the pyramids? There were pictures in books of that.

The pharaoh's eyes narrowed and what would have been anger used on battling Phoenicians, instead turned into a Nile of tears, Mississippis of sad crying. He had had so much time to think about wrong and right, he said. His tears flooded out of his eyes, he was stammering, "What happened to my Africa... What has happened to..." and the floor was becoming a swimming pool, a lake, and an ocean of the pharaoh's crying.

He was splashing explaining desperately, "No, no! America is 'All Men Are Created Equal!' We believe in these things! We...Listen, you've got to—" but the pharaoh was already underneath salt waves down below, while he was rising on the tears of history. He splashed on the waves. He already tired, he knew it wouldn't be long. He was being pulled by the sea, and if it wasn't for the sofa appearing up next to him he would have drowned. He held onto it and it took a while before he could wearily crawl on.

Chapter 65
ALICE AGAIN

Alice went by him again, swimming after a mouse. Her adventures were just beginning. "Watch out for the Queen of Hearts!" he warned her as his sofa swept him past. He wasn't sure if she heard him or saw him and she was gone before he could call to her again. He knew he was falling asleep. From a sofa in a sea of pharaoh tears, he arrived back on the surface of Earth on a river. A balloon was hovering overhead and a voice of 1000 movie stars was calling him to wake up.

Chapter 66
1956 GLASS

The balloon was anchored to the ground by a long yellow rope.

She had mastered the hula-hoop. It spun like the Saturn rings around her. She was back to wearing yellow with an Adlai Stevenson button. The transistor radio in the grass at her feet was playing Delta blues. She was waiting for him to wake up.

He was still asleep on the sofa's waterlogged green and red plaid upholstery. He was wearing the clothes of an Apache. His other clothes were drying on the balloon tether line. He knew about her nostalgia for America. Muddy Waters on the radio was singing about railroads and going home, as he stretched and yawned his way awake.

She let the hula-hoop whirl down

around her knees and settle in a circle at her feet. "Glory glory hallelujah!" she smiled. She was programmed for happiness.

"I've got to stop drifting off like that," he got up off the sofa and admired his clothes, damp from the sofa.

She looked different again. She was wearing roller skates. She walked through the tall yellow grass to him. She had to watch where she placed her feet so she wouldn't fall. She couldn't skate in a wildflower field so she walked very carefully as if she was made of 1956 glass.

She kissed him and he realized how much he looked forward to the shocks she gave him. She tied another feather in his hair. She still had five white bird feathers left. "Let's go look at the ruins." She took him by the hand, leaving the transistor playing piano in the grass.

Chapter 67
THE RUINS OF
THE LAND
ONCE ALIVE

Like a curled sleeping cat, the ruins were quiet circles, stones where once there had been. She kneeled down in front of the first pile of rocks they came to and he followed her. "This is very sacred here. You can feel it, something inside the ground." She lay her hand on the earth and spread her fingers. There were clovers that came up between her fingers. The rocks had been living with moss for a long time, outlining where houses had once been.

He could feel it too: a tingling from the ground, like the wind that tells you summer is ending and fall is hanging in the trees like tigers. He put his hand on the bare round of her knee and said, "They used to live here?"

The wind blew through her hair. "Look, there are more too," she stood up and took him the fifty feet to the next mounds of stone. "I was exploring while you slept." A flock of birds startled their way into the air as they approached. "This must have been a whole town. See..." Among the stones, circles left as chalky as circus sawdust echoes. She put her last five feathers like a handprint of birds in the middle of a circle.

He wondered what kind of a robot she was, not to be like most people.

He was afraid to ask what had happened to them.

She heard the sound of something long before he did. "There's someone walking this way." On the other side of a canyon, she pointed, "See?"

His eyes went down the smooth of her arm to her finger, beyond, into the blue distance where a dot was moving, getting larger.

Chapter 68
NOSTALGIA

She shaded her eyes with her hands.

A river went through the canyon below, loud rapids.

She spun a finger in her dark hair as she waited.

It was only a very small quiet shape, with a dust cloud trailing. It neared them slowly.

Scraping along and pulled by a rope, the billionaire animal collector was dragging the carriage towards the steep edge of the other side of the canyon. When he spotted them, he stopped in the dust and called.

They were too far away, they couldn't understand him. She could only translate the meaning as she calculated with her binoculars eyes. She watched the words as they were formed. "He is saying how he has   lost

everything he owned...the prisoners escaped...
and he is powerless..."

The dot began to move again, pulling
the gold carriage. Just barely over the crash of
water they could hear him move along.

Chapter 69
AT THE EDGE
OF AMERICA

They were sitting on the flat edge of the land with their legs dangling over in the coolness of nothing. Where all Manifest Destinies ended and America with nothing left to conquer slipped off the edge and fell away; they were on the last standing rock and at their side a 1951 orchestra strung fishing lines of opera out across the abyss. She wanted to show him this waterfall, where it all ended, because she thought he would be interested. But she didn't feel like him, that losing a country was losing yourself. She could see it all as history: America really was nothing more than just time and sand that filled an hourglass for a moment. He watched all things of America, all of its history, all its brief television moments pile over the edge...He could see everything from the beginning—he pointed out the blood ship of Columbus chasing gold, and hundreds of years and people appeared and were gone...He felt the loss of it as it went underneath. Then he saw himself, not as himself, but as bright memories. Everything he had known: a purple thunderstorm with the lightning of a summer night, the buzz of airships in the stars, a game of chase in the tall grass, summers with oceans, white cold winters, everything spinning away past him. Seeing the disappearance of all the shadows of America, himself a part of the fall, that was it and he had seen enough. He didn't want to see anymore of America falling and so she took his hand, led him back to the roped balloon. He was silent and she untied the lines and they went the opposite way, as America crashed off the edge behind them.

Chapter 70
THE MOMENT
THAT
WATERFALLED

He used to have a kite hanging from his ceiling like a spider had caught and papered it there. At night…when cars passed in the streets, the lights from their moving would cross the walls and get stuck and glow on that kite for a second, coloring it blue. He used to watch that kite before he fell asleep. Nights of thunder and lightning were rare, he liked those nights most of all. He could see out the glass across the trees, into the cloudy distance where the lightning storm bumped. He would count the seconds after the lightning flashed—the seconds before the thunder were miles to be calculated—and this meant the storm was either closing in on him or leaving towards someone else.

Counting, from the blink of lightning in his room, he would drift off to sleep when the storm was leaving its rain behind to water his roof.

When he saw that stormy night die again, a moment he may have forgotten until he watched it lost, that had been him crashing with America. He turned his attention to the balloon bag above and refused to look below until they were far away so he could forget the flat edge of America falling.

Chapter 71
DICTATORS AND BUTTERFLIES

"I'm sorry." She rubbed him with her hand. "I didn't know you would react that way. I thought you would want to see it."

He had not talked to her for an hour, silently looking at the stars, not even imagining all the planets just like this, not even thinking of anything—trying not to think about that end of America.

"I'll tell you something," she cuddled him closer. He was comforted by the neon warm wires inside of her.

"I knew you would show up someday. I expected you'd be arriving with the butterflies. They show up when the spring is warmest, just before you know it's summer. Orange Bagdad Butterflies can be seen far out over the ocean, a thin colored cloud approaching and that comes closer and closer and bigger until they are there and everything is made orange. They hang to everything and climb on you and hold to your clothes. It's a legend in this part of Panama that their wings...if you listen carefully to them... they can answer your questions...they can tell your fortune. So, as they flew all around me, on my face, next to my ears, I stood very still and listened. And they told me about you...It's true."

"Good..."

America had turned Central America into a long reign of dictators, but there she was waiting for him in Panama knowing from butterflies that he would appear.

Chapter 72
SUNKEN
NURSERY RHYME

They drifted along the edges of a great ocean. Down hundreds of feet of ballooned air, they saw three wooden boats with full gray sails skirting the edge of the coast. Familiar from children's history books, he was about to name them when she did. Like a grade school nursery rhyme, she sang, "The Nina, The Pinta and The Santa Maria!" This was when they materialized America. The balloon was a perfect cinema seat to watch it happen.

The three sailing ships discovered a large harbor and drifted in to drop anchor. It was dark green deep water, clear and wide between the rocky shores. Seagulls flew around the masts of the first sailing ships and there were bound to be people watching from the forests, he thought.

Three anchors splashed into the water. He could imagine the shadows of skyscrapers waiting a couple hundred years in the future. The water would soon become brown reflecting them. Small rowboats went over the wooden sides to carry them to land.

Far above he sighed and she said, "Looks like America's been discovered."

But all that changed. The water churned into a fury of white splashing.

Whales crashed into the wooden beams of the boats, easily smashing them to pieces and the wreckage and people sunk to the oysters at the bottom of the bay. The whales flapped their tails loudly against the waves and disappeared back out to sea and the land breathed a sigh of relief.

Over them, the three president heads billowing blue sparks and coal smoke went crashing down into the horizon of sea. There was an explosion like an orange 1945 flash and they covered their eyes and felt the heat all this way away from America having never been.

Chapter 73
ANOTHER NORTH DAKOTA

In another North Dakota of the late 20th century, cars were slowing to see the police crowding around. An ambulance siren was showing up, too late for lifesaving, to park next to the curb.

Halloween teenagers costumed as horror movies stopped to ask what happened. "What's going on?" asked a Dracula at the wheel. Red ran out the corners of his mouth and a beer bottle was hidden down between his calves.

"Watch the news if you want to know," said the policeman. "Keep moving. Don't block the flow of traffic." He waved them on and spoke into his walkie-talkie.

The kids in their yellow Ford drove back into the lane of cars on their way to a 7-11.

The ambulance crew had the dead man on a stretcher, covered with a white sheet. They lifted him up into the back of the van. To save face for the Police department, he could be diagnosed dead from the poison of an insect, (the bullet lodged in his spine could be forgotten).

North Dakota got colder that evening. Snow briefly floated down sometime after three in the morning, enough to be like sugar on the heelless shoe in the dead man's garden.

His wife, his widow, was wide awake at The Holiday Inn, staring at the red carpet, wondering just what to do next. Wondering just how she would go on.

Chapter 74
MARK TWAINS

Mark Twains of slow clouds riverboated below them. Since the blue whales had shipwrecked the hopes of America being discovered by plunderers, they kept up a vigil along with the rest of the thousands of once zooed, endangered and extinct beings. All along the coastlines, the continent was protected. The Mayflower was sunk by a plesiosaur and Miles Standish wearing armor plating sunk straight to the bottom like a typewriter overboard. The map makers of Asia and Europe concluded that the world really was flat, that their ships were sinking off the edge, ending somewhere far out to sea, where the waves carried people off the planet and gone. There were millions of people living across the land, but they didn't want to create nuclear power plants, or prisons and minimum wage. In the way they were taking care of the land, things were revolving. Because of his entrapment at the zoo, he was recognized by his fellow endangered creatures. America had returned to another beginning. Their balloon became a well known landmark for the sky; birds and flying reptiles would dip their wings as they passed.

Chapter 75
WIDOW'S WALK

Meanwhile, in a different North Dakota, she was burying her dead. In a graveyard, shadowed by smokestacks clouding the sky and loud noises, the hissings and clanking of machinery at work, she was standing over a filled-in hole. Traffic on the other side of the hedge passed. The sounds from the nearby airport of planes landing and taking off rushed over her. Her husband lay under the soil and she was whispering to him, believing that he was still somewhere nearby and could hear her:

"I'm sorry...I wish you didn't go and do all that..." She was wearing black mourning. "The anger I felt, it doesn't change anything, now I've lost everything." She listened to the birds for a while. "I'm living at a hotel right now, you know. The cook said he could put me up for a while at his place. But I can't, I have to be alone for a while, you know. I'm not really sure what to do right now. It's all so sudden. I've never been alone like this before..."

She talked to her husband underground like this for a long time. Then she stood. She was silent until she was aware of all the noise around her again. And then she returned to the hotel.

Everything she owned was hanging up in the closet—her Halloween Florence Nightingale costume. She turned on the television for company.

She watched the news and saw the story of her husband again. A still photo of the factory he worked at, and a voice-over describing what he had done. A photo of their house flashed on the TV screen. She remembered the colors and the garden walkway. The cameras dramatized the story, moving from the char. A close-up of the car tires explained that he stopped at the movie theater. The camera moved again, as he must have gone, into the film's light to a seat in the balcony. "When the film ended," the reporter in front of the theater twisted his arm next to the exit, "He came out over there, in a manner Officer Don Jones found suspicious." And then there was an interview with her. She watched herself on TV like this was a mirror and she answered their questions.

Chapter 76
REAMERICA

"Here we are now," he said, "This is where I wanted us to be." He found his place and she had settled too. She was glad to be who she was and to have him with her there.

There, next to the water, on the white limestone cliff wall of the beach, he wanted to build New Hollywood, a movie screen made of stone.

He pictured what the polished rock cliff would become, with rows of granite blocks for seats, facing the beautiful stone screen. Water would come up around them, down at low tide.

They would have a curtain of ivy and flowers to pull aside.

Before the film began, the screen would shine from the moon and stars.

She would help him build a magic lantern projector and they would remake *Casablanca* out of beeswax and honey celluloid. They'd film it together and work days and nights until it was done.

A flock of dodos searched across the stones for limpets that crept ashore with the tide. And Bagdad Butterflies of Panama returned every year to rest on the movie screen.

10 PM   March 26, 1989

with Django Reinhardt's 1937 guitar

played like the propellers of the Golden Age

I worked on this book for two years after I finished the draft in 1989. It went through a few title changes: TWO STORIES FROM THE GROUND featuring *All Was Said and Done in Hieroglyphics* and *Everything That Was Done Was Done Quietly*…to the name IN TWO WONDERLANDS, until I finally marked the manuscript: THE EDGE OF AMERICA, with *Bagdad Butterfly of Panama*, and *Waterstories*, "Finished Finally, April 1991."

COVER

TWO STORIES
FROM THE GROUND
ALLEN FROST

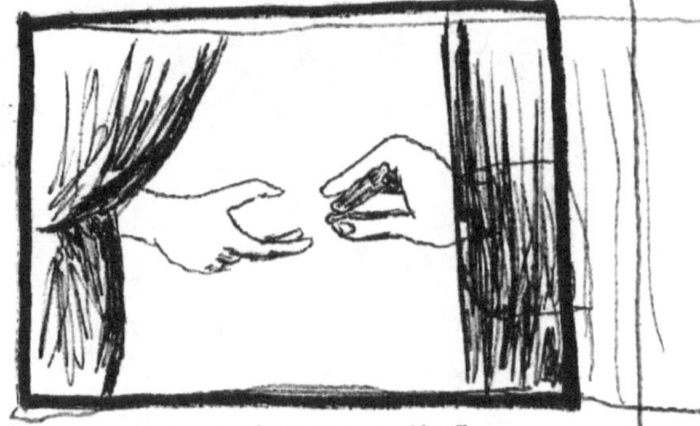

TWO STORIES
FROM THE GROUND

ALL WAS SAID AND DONE
IN HIEROGLYPHICS

EVERYTHING THAT WAS
DONE WAS DONE QUIETLY

BY ALLEN FROST

TITLE PAGE

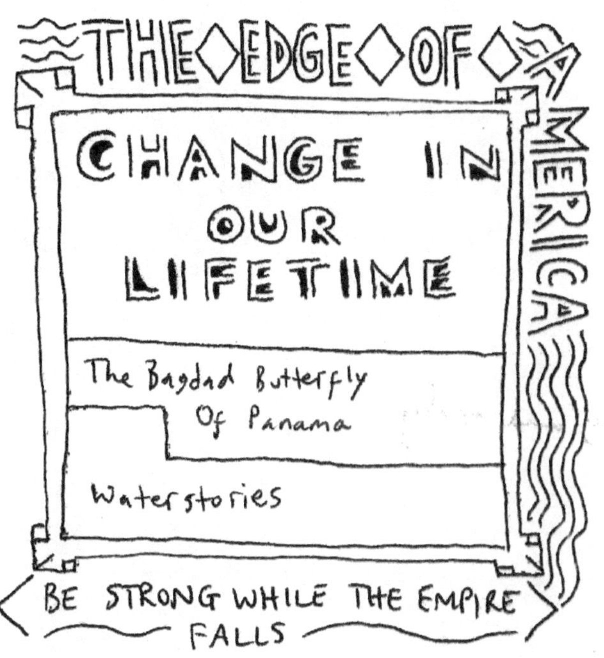

THE EDGE OF AMERICA
CHANGE IN OUR LIFETIME
The Bagdad Butterfly Of Panama
Water stories
BE STRONG WHILE THE EMPIRE FALLS

WATERSTORIES

a tragedy of seashells

the fireplace arlington

the rain in the shine
of 'no vacancy' neon

there were flowers
and also sandwiches

how she was captured
on film

15 mph from god

socialist photographers

walt whitman's
sunken treasure

the stone memory
of her moving

her reflection in ice

george washington
to the rescue

the rediscovery
of good

waxwater rockets

the first clue

a clue leads to
trouble

reconsidering

the blinking mirror

the moving of the trees
he ran

airwaves

the island seed

in the dream she had

everything that was done
was done quietly

black coffee

the atmosphere

watching

the monster

hands

broken

a tragedy
of closing doors

down
the rabbit hole

PART ONE
SLEEPY HOLLOW
UNDERWATER

A Tragedy of Seashells

It began with her underwater. Not far from the bridge, in a pond, through a hole in the ice, so blue-cold that her skin and the steel of her skates were the same.

It was raining. She was a frozen photograph under the ice. Last night when he was finally able to sleep, the cold vision of her creaked like a rocking chair far below the surface of the deep river. He dreamed she was still alive underneath, reaching up for him.

In the morning, something told him to drive and he would find her. She would show him the way. She needed to be with him again. So he got in his car and went looking.

The bridge arched its back over the river like a black metal cat hissing with wind through its suspension wire whiskers. Red and green lights strung along it, far up into the tall ice at the top. Shining at night, the bridge looked as if a Christmas tree fell across the shallow water separating the town from the forest.

Two signboards posted before the bridge where the girders turned into cement were *Revival And Salvation* (black letters on a white background with a simple-looking cross) and *Proof Through The Night* (with a waving American flag). They were signs for lost souls.

Driving over was like holding his breath, how the land dropped into the river then got out wet on the forest side, ground rising to meet him once again.

From the bridge, he could see all the land and all the things man has done to it.

The river looked up from the stone bed. The rain moved silent movie stars flickering across his windows. His car was cold, the heater was on but not working and he wore a thick green coat, a red hat and gloves. His breath showed in the air.

The radio was broken too. All he could hear was the noise the car made as it moved (engine, tires on bridge slats and the winter slipstream wind). Slowly, he found himself putting himself somewhere else; he was living in a dreamland now. He could hear himself thinking loudly, with photographs of what was memory shuffling.

If time could just be picked up and moved the way a river can jump its banks to change its course.

To wake some sense into everything disappearing, he opened the window to a splash of cold air thrown in his face. It made him gasp for breath, his eyes teared. He rolled the window up again and blinked.

The bridge was still there but it was ready to snake its tail into the ground to lie there like a fossil. Caught in the girders, a patch of blue in the white sky reminded him of summer.

He remembered the hot wind rushing

the air, with his window open so he could hear the insect electricity, the buzz up there in the tall steel, the moving of hummingspiders. Calling across miles, they could be heard luring attraction to hummingbirds who spun in and became entrapped in the webs.

But now it was winter, and the bridge disappeared with a roar into the ground, as he steered through the rain along the highway skirting the river.

The feeling came back and he thought of her dying in Winter. She will become ice, her blood, her eyes, she will freeze like a crystal under the earth.

The rain was barely melting the snow packed in animal shapes on the tar.

He passed the cemetery where the green holding stones together was eroding steeply into the river. He was scared to see the tumble of graves into water, with only the tips of stones remaining above the flood. Ghosts would be washed straight to the ocean where they would echo between the deep swimming whales.

He breathed a sigh of relief when the cemetery passed him.

He drove on by the Waxwater's, seeing their swimming pool with a miniature volcano island in the middle.

He was squinting at the outside through the windshield, looking for something from his dream, when it appeared. Why a tree, reaching from the wet ground, made him remember her, and know it was her, can be followed back to the beginning.

From the first, she was always part of the water. Here is how she first appeared: with her hands held like seashells, cupped, behind the soft of her back where it curved. He could have listened to them and heard waves. He could have pressed his ear to the shape of her hands and heard the ocean. She sold postcards in a shop next to the river and he fell in love when she moved past the postcard stand. It spun a little with her leg and arm. As her hip brushed into him, her electricity went through him and moved the pictures of seashores and famous buildings, rivers and bridges and civil war monuments, and all the messages people would ever write on them lived in the way she moved and smiled back.

He imagined her hands again and again as he drove through the rain. Held like seashells, the slender move into wrists and into her arms, on into her, like there was something soft as water running in her skin.

Of course, he still saw her in everything that was beautiful, all around, and she didn't like it being underground. Without her, thinking of her, he saw her arm appear in front of him waving for help.

He stomped the brake, the car screeched, the tires locked and squealed, but he only saw what passed by from out of his dream, into the reality of a highway tree. In his vision, there had also been the bridge further in the distance, directing him. It all added up and clicked like a camera.

A small green tree, an evergreen stood out in the ice, with white plastic bags and fastfood wrappers tangling its branches like ornaments. A small Christmas tree with a curve like her arm.

The bridge sort of shimmered in the rain beyond.

He ran for her as if she may disappear at any moment and he felt around her and found as he pulled that she could be lifted out and alive.

Another car stopped not far ahead of him. The door flew open. It was raining hard.

The Fireplace Arlington

The other car held another story. He was also haunted. He grew up with heroes lining the fireplace mantelpiece like monuments in frames. The faces began with The Indian Wars, then The Revolutionary War, The Indian Wars, The War of 1812, more Indian Wars, The Civil War, the last Indian Wars, The Spanish American War, World War One, World War Two, Korea and Vietnam...Each one of them was a death in battle; it was a history of war heroes. It was their family tradition, televisioned into them. Every generation had a war hero. It was the family honor, instant martyrdom, and immortality to be on the mantelpiece, forever kept alive. There was also an eternal flame burning in the fireplace. That was a device a relative built and enjoyed in the last few days before he went down with the Titanic. The flame was a ghostly blue around a middle flicker of gold. It would always burn in the fireplace under the photographs, like a sacred tribal burial ground.

But he wasn't accepted by the army and in his desperation, it looked like he could never be in a great war. During the Reagan years the threat loomed large and he could have been killed anywhere from the Middle East to Africa to Central America, to anywhere there was American money. But he failed the physical examination. There was plenty of opportunity for appearing on the mantelpiece, but he couldn't get in uniform.

So he became a security officer. They were very impressed with him at Associated American Grocers; he drilled his movements like inspection, drove himself like Patton between the produce aisles. This was a long way from heroic, but he always searched for the opportunity to find it.

It took a long time and then it happened. While he was driving to work, on the other side of the road, pulled over, he discovered it—his immortality.

The Rain in the Shine of 'No Vacancy' Neon

His eyes weren't seeing what was there. He could see the shape of her arm and her hand was up to his chin as he pulled. Rain was stinging against his shoulders and neck, but he was determined to free her.

Then she was out, and all of her crashed against him, mud covering him and splashing his eyes. "I've got you," he said. He held her close and carried her to the car. There was bark biting into his hands, but he felt her skin. He was gone deep into dreaming. The real world disappeared.

To him there was no man rushing to attack him. Instead, the smack against the windshield fifteen seconds later wouldn't be.

There Were Flowers and Also Sandwiches

Only seconds from his heroic moment, he remembered the celebration when his uncle died in Vietnam. Flags were flown tremendously at half mast on the porch for weeks of rain. He remembered the wet steep grass of the cemetery that morning. There even seemed to be fog across the road that morning. More than anything else on that day was the ceremonial adding of the photo to the family tree of heroes that grew with war. There was a glow in that room, a heavenly pumpkin of gold and orange light in the living room, and the furniture was all fiery with swirled design and there, being advanced to the height above the fire, was a new inspiration. There was even a smell, still in his memory, of that day. There were flowers and also sandwiches.

It glowed strongly in his memory and it also haunted him as a ghost at night, inviting him to step up closer, into the frame.

It was the only way to write himself into the family history, but he seemed to be failing. He wore the security officer uniform constantly, never knowing when he would have to be called into action. He would always be ready to die in uniform.

At the Sears in town he got a photograph taken and his face under the hat braiding was MacArthur returning to the Philippines: this was the photo he wanted displayed on the mantelpiece when it became his time. He framed the photo in gold and put it in an envelope marked *To Be Opened Upon Death*. It was pushed under the folded socks in his drawer.

He dreamed of his glorious death (with his uniform hung on a hook close to his bed) every night was a new twist that would never fail to leave him dying in a blaze of bullets.

Though he was not issued a gun for surveillance of the grocery store, he carried his father's world war pistol, greased with the smell and shine of that death on Omaha beach. Sometimes he practiced spinning the gun on his shooting finger as he imagined his gunslinger cowboy ancestor in the middle photo, brown with the dust of the Old West. He bought special bullets for the gun, designed to penetrate steel, because he was never sure how death would face him. Death could be tempting him with a bulletproof vest, but he was ready; it would be tooth for a tooth.

He even walked like a John Wayne movie. But every night at the supermarket, it was the same, just rows of soup and detergents and nothing but stillness among all the food. Sometimes he'd turn off all the lights and sit in the dark by the unlocked door, tempting someone to enter and give him over to the mantelpiece. Even though it wasn't the navy, or air force, army or marines, he was happy doing the job, anticipating glory. A huge supermarket at night. Candy, coffee, batteries, fruits and vegetables, were a friendly audience. The aisles could be darkened with the light switch, then he could play the muzak tape and syrupy music would fill the store.

He loved to wander down the aisles in the dark with Top 40 violins creating an environment of Eden for him. Sometimes it lulled him to sleep. Once he slept for two hours in lettuce. Lettuce glowed at his flashlight the color of the mantelpiece marble. It was not like a submarine, fighter plane or tank, but it was his supermarket and he commandeered it like a late night war general.

With such a legacy of heroes, he took every chance he could of martyring himself. Once he pulled a little girl out of the way of a speeding car, careful to set her on the sidewalk as the bumper broke both his legs and arms and set him in hospital traction. He could see his photo ever closing the gap towards the mantle. But it retreated as his condition bettered and he was walking with crutches finally, then fine. He had seen such a glow in his relatives' eyes as they paused over his crushed body, but as he got better, they lost hopes and stopped coming to see him, stopped sending flowers.

It was so important for him to stake his life on a heroic end. Sometimes he was just trouble-making though. As his car slid to a halt in the rain and he ran out in his security officer uniform (blue with orange and white striped trim and the belt with a flashlight and twenty keys) he was definitely thinking of saving the world and sending himself to the mantelpiece.

The thief with the tree seemed oblivious and that made him angry. It made him wish he had a siren and lights on his car.

He was slipping in the mud as he ran

and slid onto his knee, but he was up at once and looking half at the man lifting a tree out of the ground and half at his stained blue clothes. Looking less than heroic now—he imagined his dead uncle in Vietnam in a uniform shining with medals and the only mar was a tear of blood pooled into a button shape of cloth and he was dead and glorified in the halo colors of the mantelpiece.

As his feet splashed through the wet grass, a Patsy Cline muzak song was trodding him on with its swelling violins.

How She Was Captured
On Film

He lay her down on the back seat. Her arm held towards him. She was so glad to be alive. He had to move her feet while he shut the door and got behind the wheel. She laughed and reached out to touch his neck.

Smiling away, he drove smack into the running uniformed man who suddenly appeared out of the blur of bridge and rain.

15 MPH from God

They said he couldn't have felt a thing. The impact came so suddenly, he couldn't have realized what happened. The doctor informed the relatives gathered at the door that he had died painlessly in his sleep during the night. The response of the family to the news their son was dead from the impact of a car going fifteen miles per hour (why was he there?) struck into a coma and death painlessly, was horror.

The echoes of their cries carried home to the fireplace, where the photos shook and a crack soared up from them, along the wall. But worst of all, the eternal flame burned out, hissing up a smoky last word.

In the attic, a saber in a sea chest rattled and punched its silver tip through the wood.

The doctor recommended a priest to talk

about their grief, but but the dead son's father calmly explained, they had no God anymore.

Socialist Photographers

The family was disintegrating (they hardly knew each other anymore). Generation gaps and silences. They were the end of the family in America. Their fireplace mantle was collapsing, splintering, looking like a graveyard robbery and the photos were blanketing in dust and cobwebs and an insect with twelve legs was living on the portrait of a man killed at Harper's Ferry. A rainbow of cracked plaster. Their house was the Great Depression, it was *The Grapes Of Wrath*. People would see in the family haunting gray black and white stillness, sense in them the words of Lenin, Marx and Engels and then there would be great gatherings of speeches and music where Woody Guthrie, Leadbelly, Cisco Houston and Pete Seger would be singing to downtrodden crowds in overalls in their backyard and the police would crush them with clubs, and dogs would be snarling, and "the Reds" would be singled out and killed, attacked and jailed and this would go on for years. Until the invention of apathy.

Walt Whitman's Sunken Treasure

When he was buried by the river, the day was raining and the relatives were dressed in black, shadows of umbrellas on their wet feet.

The supermarket sent a huge horseshoe shape of flowers with a quote from Walt Whitman wrapped around carnations. The bouquet was resting at the head of a disappearing hole in the ground like the marker for a sunken ship. *To A Truly Great Employee, Who Will Be Missed* was written on the sash, weaved between the colors of all the flowers, and the family remained not quite the statues they were. They were coming to life again gradually, reading the message. The words were promising, perhaps they had been wrong about him, maybe he had been a hero, "A Truly Great Employee."

They held hands around the foot of the grave and they let last farewell flowers, dropped onto the soil, settle for a moment, before they left for home.

They drove in a caravan of headlights through the town, back to a house where even though it was raining hard, the lawn sprinklers were showering puddles in the grass. A lake was beginning to fill in the space around their house, past ankle deep, with the thousand tears of ancestors.

The cars slid into the water and stopped. Big waves crashed from them onto the steps of the porch. And all the mourners waded out of their cars with their umbrellas held overhead, went ashore, onto the porch and in the door.

Inside was also filling with water. All the faucets were on and pouring. Upstairs, the bathtub was sending a waterfall down the flower pattern carpeted stairs.

They took their seats on chairs and

couches and two women decided to splash through into the kitchen to make coffee and tea.

An old woman rocked in the colonial rocking chair, slow waterwheeling, while she stared blankly at the fireplace mantelpiece and the photos that were upon it. Generations of war heroes would be drowning before long. The Arlington Titanic was striking an iceberg.

The Stone Memory
of Her Moving

After the police and their loud, blinding colored lights had sirened away from the site of the 15 mph tragedy, he was driving home with the tree of her in his backseat singing him the song on the radio.

The rain was driving the land into the river. Muddy streams were pouring down the hills across the road. Foundations were slipping. Passing by the cemetery, he happened to look over there (not wanting to, but doing it anyway) and he saw headstones sliding towards the river like dominoes falling. And he saw her stone (what was left of her above ground) only yards from the torrents of water. Immediately, like the shadow of a blown out candle, he swung to the cemetery and with a blink he was there, driving across the grass, avoiding all the headstones and monuments and flower wreathes drenched in rain. At the edge of the cemetery, stones toppled over into the river like slow motion train disasters.

He stopped the car and he got out into the rain. He pulled the tree from the backseat. Now it was only a tree (her arm, not an arm, just a trunk and branches and green needles) and he had to save what was her resting place on Earth.

Running with the tree gripped tight, he landed on his knees by her gravestone and read her name with the desperate sadness of everything he ever knew now reduced to letters. Her name, her years of life and a poetic last sentence. He wished the tree he held was her. But the bark scratched him and the fir needles were sharp—it wasn't her he held.

The ground was moving beneath him, he was moving with the land. So he shoved the tree against her headstone, bracing the tree against the short sentences that were all that was left of her.

The branches covered the stone and he hoped it would hold her back. But the land kept moving to the river, to the sea waiting far away.

He pushed his body up against the marble and prayed to the gray sky overhead that somehow the rain would hear him and help hold her back. But all that came down to him was rain and more rain, turning the land into flowing, and it kept him and the stone memory of her, moving towards the river.

As he slid over the embankment with the marble in his arms, the weight fell onto him and kept him under the water and he couldn't resist. Closing his eyes, he was accepting of the crush of her words that trapped him in the current.

Her Reflection In Ice

Days ago…

When she was skating, she moved across the ice as if she had migrating birds pulling her along. Opening his eyes to her and closing them and opening them again, she smiled and waved at him.

He remembered his fingers, how they tumbled with the strings of his skates, how cold it was and she was wearing sweaters and wool and looked warm with her Olympics. He laughed, wished he had a gold medal to give her, and waved back to her as he started to tie his right skate up.

When he looked up, she was gone. There was a hole in the ice. She had fallen through, she was gone. There was barely a sound, barely a sigh from her as she vanished, and he was up, falling to his knees on the ice as his feet slipped from under him. Sliding to the jagged ice hole where she had disappeared, he was on his hands and knees yards away when her arm splashed through. An image for a second. When it sunk, she was gone forever.

The ice was cracking under him, water seeping through, but he felt over the edge where she had submerged. With a snap, he was in the water, splashing at the cold, shouting her name in jagged breaths across the pond until he was able to pull himself up, back onto the surface. He looked back to where she had gone. She was still gone, but he stood on the edge of the pond shouting her name, across and back across the pond until the police were there and a boat lifted her out. The reflection of ice was in her eyes. She was taken away in an ambulance.

He couldn't move. He looked at the pond, at what had turned her into a statue. Quiet now, there were pieces of floating ice and it was starting to rain harder, so he went to his car and sat inside there, looking out the windows.

He thought of all the ways this could have been different. He thought of all the things he could have done. They could have gone to a matinee film instead. A film could have saved her life. They could have had a sandwich at the diner. A toasted cheese sandwich could have saved her life. They could have, (they could have).

For some reason, ice and snow, he thought of George Washington crossing the Delaware, the heroics of that crowded wooden boat, and how America would be so different if the Delaware was a tragic river. He wished George Washington and his wooden boat had been here an hour ago.

George Washington
To The Rescue

And an hour more before (heroically)…

He was well known, well liked at his supermarket. The cashiers, the clerks and customers smiled for him as he walked down Aisle 6, Canned Goods, on his way to the vegetables. His keys and the swinging black flashlight on his belt made familiar security guard sounds. His shined boots clicked on the wax linoleum floor. He would buff it again tonight after watching Johnny Carson on the TV in the back room, then he would admire the glow of the yellow lights on the marbling floor, like it was a postcard sent from a holy tomb or museum.

He often came in during the afternoon, hours before his shift began, because he liked it here. Just to stroll around the aisles to say his hellos to people (the entire town shopped here and everyone knew him). To take a look at the lettuces down Aisle 6 made his life's days complete. The lettuces sprinkled green with wet drops of water from a hose between the spinach and celery.

He'd leave to go out for a drive after a while of talking with people who knew him. It was like watching TV with someone. And then he'd drive his car over the bridge and to the hill beyond where he would park up there like a planetarium, and watch.

He liked to drive and observe the way the land twisted and moved around his car. It would always be a peaceful driving day, even if it was raining and there was snow on the ground.

But this afternoon the sky was the color of milk and it was not raining. His palms were tensed, knotting around the steering wheel like a man dying of thirst.

He had a feeling about this day.

He distrusted it when there was no rain. Suspicious, he knew something would happen on his ritual drive to the hill and back.

As he crossed the bridge, returning to work, it happened so fast—his car slipped out over the water with pieces of guard railing exploding all around the grill and hood. It was a long way to the water, but the water didn't wait long for the car to hit and submerge.

The car cracked through the ice sheet and skilleted to the bottom, side to side.

There were weeds on the river bottom covering the stones with green that mossed up around the frame of the car and waved. (Fish would return to examine the wreck, salmon on their way upstream would stop next to the metal.) He began to struggle inside and scared the fish away. His forehead was bleeding and he was pounding on the windows, until finally he made them budge and roll down so Arctics of water shot in. The water reached in hands and pulled him out, floated him up towards a gray halo above.

He splashed into the air and reefed himself up onto the ice, yelling clouds screamed into the air. They were echoed by someone else calling for help.

It didn't matter how he felt. He ran across the ice for the shore where the cry had flown. Through the woods, he ran towards an opening in the trees where in the gray light, he saw someone on the pond.

Someone was reaching over the broken ice for an arm held out in the water.

Running, screaming through the clearing, still streaming wet with blood from his cuts, he plummeted towards the frozen scene on the ice like a Medieval painting of a monk transfixed by a charging angel.

He didn't even slow, running so fast to the ice hole that he just dove in headfirst, back into the cold, and his eyes were searching the darkness.

A girl's arm brushed him and he grabbed her tight and swam her up with him.

"Get to a house quick and call for an ambulance!" he commanded and that other man ran through the woods to a telephone.

Her pulse was weak, but she was alive as he returned her to life with C.P.R. It was part of his training as a security guard. He was saving her life. He was still saving her life as the ambulance came and he collapsed onto the ice, perfectly dead.

The Rediscovery of Good

Like the rediscovery of good in the world, the news traveled of his heroic death. The family drove to the funeral in a slow black convertible. In front, on a carriage drawn by a horse, was his coffin. He was buried in his uniform. The supermarket attached a plaque in the lettuce and renamed Aisle 6 after him.

But more than the town's worshipping, was what his family did. There was a ceremony, sacred as a passing torch that evening. The house sat moist in the rain. The light of the moon cast in their snowy yard projected green across the walls. The only light inside came from downstairs. Behind a drawn shade, the fireplace mantelpiece was aglow with candles.

They held a photo of him between them, carried his icon to the mantelpiece where they placed him down on ribbons beside his uncle who crashed a B-52..

Their war dead from the founding of America turned to look at the newest—a security officer who died saving a girl trapped under ice. Proud space was made for him by moving all the other pictures over a bit. When the family all backed away from the fireplace, there was the eternal flame burning in the hearth.

Through the trees, back through the drip of rain, seen from back away, under the tall black shapes of sheltering fir trees, their house was beating with the ice light of purple hearts.

And under the Moon raining night, she was fine, doing well in the hospital with flowers surrounding her, there in her bed, looking like springtime. She was laughing as he read her horoscope for that day she fell into ice. "Today is your day to relax..."

Twelve years from now, she will find a

box in an attic overlooking the yard she grew up in, the field and the pond in the woods, and she will open the box and see in it the white skates. She will be so cold just looking at them that she will close the lid quickly, wondering why they had been saved, and shove the box away. She will leave the attic as quickly as possible, as if that was a Sleepy Hollow she was in.

PART TWO
HE REMEMBERED.
THERE WAS WATER
UNDERGROUND.

Waxwater Rockets

On the road on the other side of the river, Mark Twaining opposite the town just past the bridge into the woods, the people along this stretch lived with a mystery, a strange emanation moving with rain, falling through ice, that could make and unmake the passage of time, unravel and rewind what happened.

Now the bridge had a tarp wrapped over a section of the railing so no one could see if an accident occurred there or not. Below, on the river ice surface, there were boards patched and nailed together and anchored over where a car would have fallen, if a car did fall.

The people living along this side of the river were not used to things happening which couldn't be explained. There were four seasons in the forest, there was always rain for them and things could be arrived at naturally like using tree moss as a compass.

In this place caught in between, the Waxwaters lived along the road, where a tree left its imprint in the soil...or maybe it was just where a dog was digging for underground rocketry. Their dog, could easily have done it, sniffing around the woods again looking for rockets that had been shot and lost in the trees. Orville Waxwater knew they had little chance of reaching the Moon, so he coated the rockets with honey, in hopes that the dog would find and retrieve his experiments before the raccoons did.

There were rockets high up in the branches of all the trees and during storms they would fall to the ground. Winter was the season for finding rockets when the storm winds blew in from the coast and the dog searched for sweet smelling rockets buried half in the snow. Finding one, scratching around until it was freed, the dog knew how to carry it home by the other end, with the sharp nose-cone, dragging a stripe along the ground. Orville would toss it into a pile of recycled rockets and Wilbur would offer a biscuit.

But today the dog found something else, and trotted the path back to the house where Wilbur was taking a shower. The controls were made of television channels. For hotter water, he turned the channel selector, a 1950's teak wood hi-fi model soldered into spot where the hot/cold dial used to be. He twisted the 'Tint' button for a finer spray. It was so relaxing time could stand still. Once he took a shower for over an hour.

The dog was waiting outside the door with the polished badge in between her paws. When Wilbur opened the bathroom door, he would be confronting all the mystery the bridge and the road were hiding behind all that snow and rain and secrecy, under all those tarps and boards.

The First Clue

The dog looked from the badge to the door, badge to the door and when Wilbur Waxwater walked out, he couldn't believe it when he read the little shiny words. With his towel wrapped tightly around him, he stepped backwards into the shower steam. He sat on the edge of the tub to collect his thoughts.

His father had disappeared overseas. His father's name was Wilbur too and it was written *Wilbur Wright Waxwater* on a stone placed in the woods. When the boat went down, he sank with it because he couldn't swim without it. He is still at the bottom of the gray Atlantic, his arms wrapped around the steering wheel, uniting himself with it, with over forty years of coral and barnacles. What he really wanted was to be on one of those huge sailing ships that used to cross the horizon when he remembered his childhood. His son never knew his father, except by black and white ocean photos, so he got to know his father's father. He called his grandfather, "Orville!" and yelled again, "Orville!"

His grandfather was in the garage, building a submarine out of tropical seashells. Blue sparks that shot off into the air around him were landing in the snow.

Wilbur yelled once more for his help, "Orville!"

"Yes?!"

"The dog found something strange. It's a badge!"

Orville took off his goggles and went into the house, wiping his greasy hands onto his overalls. "What badge?"

"This badge." His grandson handed him the supermarket security officer badge.

Their dog was barking loudly with more than a badge to show them still. Wilbur put on his clothes quickly and they followed, out across the yard, their dog's track leading back through the wet tall snow.

A Clue Leads To Trouble

Orville was saying, as they went along bending and crunching the snow under boots, "But this is the badge from that man who died. I know his name. I read about him in the paper."

"Exactly," said Wilbur in reply, keeping with his grandfather's steps. Water was rushing off the side of one hill like the rotten lettuce water in *East Of Eden*. A James Dean sun moved in and out of the branches of the trees, hiding, spying on the two. And a freight train was running somewhere not far away.

The dog stopped at the edge of the road and called back to them as a truck rumbled by. The dog waited for them, and they all walked across the road, to the place the dog had been digging.

"This is where the badge came from."

A fountain of soil was thrown across the snow. The dog started to dig again.

Wilbur got down on his knees, swiped away at the cold dirt and stones and then his digging fingers ran into something. He drew his hand away, too horrified to speak.

"What? What is it?"

The dog was sniffing and pawing.

Orville lowered himself to the ground and clawed into the cold. He pushed the dirt out between the fingers of a hand, so cold he thought he had discovered a Civil War statue.

"I don't like this…I think we should just leave as quickly as possible." Wilbur was taking steps backwards.

"No! What would happen if we just left?"

They would have gone back across the road, back through the snow with the dog ahead running, ice-breaking a path. They would have all gone inside shivering and not speaking about what they'd felt and seen. They would put on the coffee and Orville would say something about the new waitress, the warm way she looked at Wilbur when she slipped the check onto the table. He would have laughed at the way Wilbur was pretending to have forgotten and Orville would watch him get up and go over to pour the coffee. They would have had their coffee and watched out the windows sitting there at the kitchen table. There would be a goose on the lawn. They would both have watched it silently, drinking their coffee, until the bird flew away. Then they would have both returned to their projects: the submarine and the swimming pool. Orville would have been entranced once again, applying the fish scales to the hull. Wilbur would have stood by the plastic swimming pool and stared at the island of rock and plants in the middle of the circled water. He would have pondered the island in the swimming pool for a long time and nothing would have happened to it. Both of them would have been able to forget about the earth by the road, just keep blocking it out, until finally it would disappear as a memory.

"We can't go back," Orville said. "We have to find out what this is all about."

"No, we should call the police or the news. They like this kind of thing," Wilbur was on the gravelly edge of the road, "I don't want anything to do with this. Come on, let's leave. I'll call someone."

"I'm going to find out what's going on."

"Well, I'm going back to the swimming pool." Wilbur left his grandfather, digging in the hole and crossed the road, with the dog leading the way. He looked back from across on the other side, almost expecting to see his grandfather giving up and following him home. But Orville was still digging.

"We're going to call someone," Wilbur told the dog. "Then we can figure out the swimming pool." He followed the path his dog had broken through slush and snow.

Reconsidering

When he was back at the house, he regretted leaving his grandfather with that mystery. He knew he had to go back.

The worst thing he could imagine was happening in his mind, while he started to run through the freezing and frozen water, back to the road.

There was no sign of Orville by the hole, on the road, or in the trees. He was gone. Tree branches were rattling and rubbing against each other, up where there didn't seem to be any wind. The sky was blue in places, like pond water.

The Blinking Mirror

Wilbur Wright Waxwater the Second stopped at the edge and stared. It looked deep as a wishing well. There was a wind blowing out of it, powdering the snow like a transmission from Admiral Byrd across the Arctic.

"Orville!" he screamed at the sunken earth. All he saw was water, black water like oil reflecting him back. He felt he was looking at a photo of his father down there, disappearing to the deepest abyss of the ocean, where he ended drowned under miles but still holding tight to the wheel, still in control and still clinging to it as a human-shaped coral, with fish slowly moving around him.

"Orville!" he shouted into the dark that scattered his reflection like a passing of birds. His grandfather was gone, but deep down in there somewhere, still living, he knew.

He shouted again and the surface of the water barely moved, like a mirror blinking.

He shouted the name again in every direction of the road switching back and forth like gray blades through the snow. But there wasn't the faintest reply, just the moving of the trees.

The Moving of the Trees
He Ran

He ran away from the watery pit across the tar for home. Wilbur knew what he had to do. There was a transmitter in an aquarium filled with lights and wires, glowing turquoise. He would have to make contact with a spirit using a fishbowl radio. And he had to hurry.

It took him less than three minutes running hard to get home and it took his dog even less for them to reach the door, through into the warm and dry.

He kicked his boots off into the corner and snow dripped onto the floor boards. He threw his coat on the stairway to upstairs and ran to a closet marked Radio Room.

He pulled the door open and leaped onto the chair, in front of the radio control board. When his headset was on, he clicked the lights into the dials, tapped them, and he listened to a hum come to life.

Airwaves

It didn't last long before a sound came across the airwaves, so loud he had to adjust the dials quickly down. With the arrows all pegging through the red, Wilbur heard a voice calling his name. He was afraid to answer into the microphone and could only listen.

"The swimming pool..." and it repeated like an owl again, then flew away abruptly into static.

Wilbur took off the headphones, set them on the switches, and repeated the words of the faraway echoes, "The swimming pool..." Quickly, he got back into his boots and coat from the stairs, knowing something was waiting for him in that round pool of water.

The Island Seed

Glasses were sleeping like cats in the sink. He walked through the kitchen, out the door to where the swimming pool water and ice and island were inside the blue stretched plastic.

The swimming pool was about twelve feet across and an island had been planted growing up from the bottom to surface about two feet above the water and thin ice. Warm circulating hoses kept the ice from thickening, steam was circling a chalkdust fog around the island.

Wilbur stood in the shallow snow looking at the pool, still amazed that this island all began with just a seed. Trying to figure out what made a volcano, working with earth and fire and water, he came up with a seed. (A small green seed that he had rolled between his thumb and forefinger and then dropped   like a dice to the bottom of the gambling pool.) Since two springs ago when he had planted the island, he had watched it grow from that seed to a pebble, to a stone that grew like coral, months at a time, larger and larger until it surfaced for air and started to sprout with plants.

The island was still summer green, thick with a miniature jungle even though winter cold white settled on everything else. There was a warmth and energy coming from the island that he just couldn't seem to figure out.

He had a set of thermometers, all so accurate, precise in Celsius and Fahrenheit, that he would push into the island soil, but the reason for the temperature eluded him as the water slipped through his fingers. He had charts of temperature graphs in spiral bound notebooks and he pondered them for hours every evening before going to sleep, hoping somehow a dream could illuminate it all for him.

Wilbur walked up to the swimming pool and rested his arms on the plastic edge. Looking into the water, the warm hoses humming and gurgling with their steam, bubbles pushing little ice flows back and forth.

He could also hear the faint crossing of cars on the road through the trees. On still quiet nights, the wind sounded like steel drum echoes played along the wide metal of the bridge. In summer it was almost Trinidad.

He listened to all of this and the dog starting to bark as he stared at the island. It was becoming his Titanic. But instead of sinking, it blew up.

A sudden steam shot out of the sides and split the island open like a lava fruit, blew it apart. He was sprayed with green, wet pieces torn from his island landing all over him and the white yard. Water was blasting up from the ground. And he remembered—there was water underground.

That made him laugh as he stood there. "Of course! Like Old Faithful!" Hot water droplets warmed into his skin and the dog was barking in circles. He watched the gusher with his hands shielding his eyes.

Water elevated his grandfather up through the ground towards the wintery sky. Splashing took Orville out of the Earth and he flashed out of the spray and landed in the snow, finally able to breathe again. Behind him, water was sinking back into the ground.

PART THREE
THE FALLEN LOOKING-GLASS HOUSE

In The Dream She Had

There were enough pianos to fill a lake, in the barn so big it could have slept the shadow of the bridge her father helped to build.

One window shade was open above. Its orange light was a square reflection on the smooth piano touching her. The girl rested her elbows on the red wood and stared at the patch of light and slowly she became hypnotized, looking in.

There were also clouds in that reflection. Even birds were flying in the piano wood.

Polishing her family's pianos all morning, afternoon long, made her tired and she yawned and rested her cheek down next to the window's shine.

She saw another bird go by, next to her lips, and then she closed her eyes to sleep... Wondering what an ocean tide of pianos on fire it would make if she lit the matches she had hidden in her dress pocket...And in the dream she had, she found herself trapped by a mob into the black room of pianos. She ran from the barn through shadows and dark places and quickly she was gone from them. Hiding, she watched them move into the barn and it wasn't long before they came back out the doors pushing pianos in front. Her face was careful, quiet behind the white flowers, as she watched them move pianos towards the river. Pianos, all the hundreds that her father had her so carefully keep beautiful, were dumped over the hillside into the river that roared below. All the storm was leaving only faint flickers of lightning to glitter off the polish of floating, sinking pianos. She hid there in fear inside of the flowers. She watched the months go by as the castle's burns were restored and repainted bright and hung with flags and those people returned on ferry boats to pay twenty dollars a family to see the amusement park this became.

Everything That Was Done Was Done Quietly

She lived on a river island between two lands of frozen trees. It was always warmer on the island than on the two mainlands and flowers grew in the winter. Bees flew and birds wove nests in the peach leaves.

There were still pieces of ice jigsawing water, big enough to hop across to their castle.

She was asleep in the barn, but beginning to wake up. Stretching and yawning (the reflection of window she slept in had slid off onto the floor) she got down off the piano slowly. Her blue and white dress slid like the sky. All her clothes were blue and white dresses because she was Alice In Wonderland.

But she had been dreaming and predicting a piano apocalypse, not a white rabbit adventure. That was another story.

Although she used to have a rabbit, like a magic act, he vanished. A day later he was washed up on the rocks of the shore. A morning with cool fog hiding the lands, her rabbit lay on the stones white as bone as she kneeled beside. She lifted the stiff soft fur and pulled her rabbit into a hammock of her blue dress and cradled her pet away. She made a hole in the ground and put him down inside on top of flowers plucked from the tall weeds and she covered him over. After the river washed across those banks and took back her rabbit along with earth and flowers, she began to realize the power that moved in the water underneath the bridge.

Her family made its fortune with that bridge. Her father designed it, its shape and its metal. The metal was something he invented to last forever. During World War Two, the navy built ships out of the metal. He promised them it was a Ghostdance steel, that it could deflect bullets and bombs. By now his war metal was far below ocean waves, or lying rust in tall weeds, and people were worried about their bridge. Rainwater ran through holes in places.

But his fortune remained solid, he built an island estate with a view. His bridge was always in sight and as it crumbled with time, so did he. She moved through the room like a ghost. She never asked him why he bought so many pianos with his fortune. If she did ask, she'd have to ask with her hands. Deaf, everything she did was done quietly.

Black Coffee

She watched him from the high window, as he was guided by two nurses along the flowered path. When he was able to get away from them, he would stand on the beach and scream at the bridge, "I never should have made you!"

She could only see him as a small drawn figure, with arms flailing at the river.

His footsteps were slowly laid down, as he was led back inside. The nurses were patient. They knew this was something he would do and all they could do was gather him back with black coffee inside the castle.

The Atmosphere

Her life was spelled out simply in the way she looked out windows. She was born on the island eight years ago and she never left it. She gazed out the window like she had an idea she never would. He didn't want her to leave the island, her father wanted her to be safe. She never heard the sounds of everything all around her, a silent movie playing for eight years. Days were long sad filled hours of pianos.

In the summer, boats went by as if they were painted on the river and she was in a museum, made of glass. In the winter, the river was iced over and the trees were covered in snow and water. She spent hours of the day watching. Not just across the river and into the trees, she also looked into the sky at night. She had a silver telescope on the window sill. Venus was her favorite planet, a tiny far away drop of green water light in the stars.

Watching, slowly and noticeably, the bridge was collapsing. Pieces of it were falling off to the river, leaving rusted missing orange scars on the once sleek black and miracle metal. That's what her father spent the days of the years watching.

Alice and he could only watch.

The Monster

Cars driving across the bridge would loosen metal and make it fall. More and more of the bridge was being patched to hold it together. There was a disaster waiting to occur and it all depended on a matter of time. People held their breath when they crossed the bridge and kept their eyes fixed hopefully on the other side. Prayers were always made before and after crossing it, but it would take a stormy night of wind, thunder and lightning for the town to finally react.

The bridge was a symptom of it all. It seemed the whole of the town was changing and falling apart. Where there used to be trees in so many numbers, now there stood only two at the end of a mall parking lot. Things were dying underneath tar and cement. Rain couldn't feed the seeds and roots anymore.

People watched it all occur, with hope sinking away in their eyes, as what happened to the land was happening to them. No one knew for sure who was doing this, but it felt like a war on life. There were no good jobs, and the jobs people had were working them to death. They were losing, but somebody somewhere must be winning—somebody with their money, never seeing or feeling this effect.

While everything they used to know was disappearing, they decided who that somebody must be and they were waiting for the signal to hunt him down. Everyone knew who created the bridge with all its faults. He lived on the castle island rising its gray walls out of the river. He was never seen in town anymore, not for many years, but his photo was run in the newspaper like a wanted man. The paper demanded that he use his riches to repair and rebuild the bridge before there was nothing left. But there was only silence from the island.

People cursed the bridge, the island, and the twenty five year old photo of that inventor. People knew little about him: he married a fortuneteller and he had a deaf daughter. His wife left him and he stayed walled on the island ever since.

They imagined his back turned to the bridge, with all the town's money in his bank. Rumors spread, crept from house to house at night, until faster and faster, he became a monster.

Hands

Quietly, it started on the horizon where the clouds were dark and moving closer as evening began. Wind started to move the trees, and waves chopped the river. Birds flew together to find shelter. Distant sounds of thunder funneled up along the shores and rattled the panes of window glass on the island. The rain had been driven off into the woods by the wind from black storm clouds.

As Alice in the castle looked out, the window shook and lightning flashed in front of her palms on the glass, she felt the storm almost here. The waves below threw themselves white onto the rocks of the island.

Her bedroom lights were turned off, she didn't notice the electricity go out, the wires were down. The nurses rushed to get torches and candles from closets.

Alice watched the bridge swaying, lit up by branches of lightning. A tree burst into flame and crashed down into the water.

Upstairs, in the wind of the turret outside, her father was holding the bridge up between his outstretched hands, shouting, "Don't fall! Don't fall!"

Broken

Up where he could feel the thunder and wind, the lightning pierced through his shadows. Its white fierce light snapped out of the black. He saw the bridge between his held out hands shake. His voice shot across the rocks and water to the steel buckling bridge and he commanded it to hold.

He saw suspension wires straining, and lightning bolting into the river around, while he shouted again.

Behind him, the trapdoor sprang open and torch lights led two, then three of the housekeepers up onto the stones where they heard him screaming.

There he was, holding his hands before his face, with the light from their flames across his back. He leaned into the wind, his body bending over the edge and they thought he was going to jump.

As he strained to hold his hands around the bridge, they pulled at his arms from behind and fought with his body that had become like iron. When they broke him and brought his arms down against his sides, he watched the bridge explode into pieces. Lightning shot into it and the wind tore it all loose and into the water.

The sound of the collapse sent loud terror for miles in every direction as they dragged him down through the trapdoor.

A Tragedy of Closing Doors

The town without electricity jumped at the sound of the falling bridge. Headlights took all the people to the river to see the crumpled wreckage of metal lit up between thunder.

The way they hissed among themselves, it was decided upon quickly and boats were gathered along the shore. Torches were made out of tree branches to light the way to the island where their anger and revenge was directed.

As she watched out her tall window, the dots of bright flaming light began to cross and she ran to her closet to hide.

Paddling, rowing, sailing and motoring they came across the choppy cold river with torches and clubs and guns held in their hands.

The old inventor bridge builder was

collapsed under bedsheets and blankets pulled tightly over him. He was so quiet now, with the candles beside him flickering, left alone to sleep.

A hundred people came ashore and formed a fiery spot with their flashlights and torches and swarmed along the stone walls to the castle doors. Dark windows looked down on them as they pressed together at the oak doors, broke them open into a checkered hall that echoed all their footsteps and reflected their flames shining off oil paintings hung on the walls.

Through the hallway their shadows coursed, under an arch that took them winding up stairs.

What the servants could hear and run from, Alice imagined in her hiding.

Her father was frozen, lying in bed, in such a complete quiet nothing could disturb. Candles next to him slowly melted and their light waved with a rush of wind approaching.

Doors were crashing open, up and down the halls, as they searched for him. Shouting back and forth as they searched rooms full of covered furniture and dusty book shelves and windows reflecting themselves back.

Alice saw light under her door and pushed aside a sliding panel next to her. She was gone through as they tore her room apart looking for him.

They found what was him in a garden of candles. He was in the form of an old man, so much older and fallen alone than his photo in the newspaper. Hands grabbed him and shook him as more people poured into the room, surrounded the bed with torches and their curses. Flame caught hold of the blankets and they all backed away. He made no sound. They stayed only long enough to see his life disappear. Then they were shouting for more and looting as they went. Paintings, candlesticks, lamps and furniture, whatever else could be carried as they ran.

She dropped down from behind a gold framed landscape painting into a huge room of pianos. On the wood of the pianos, orange flames slid glowing and she could make her way through by their shine. She followed a path in shadow between them to the door.

Slowly she pushed it open and she could see people running away with what wasn't theirs. Two men carried a chandelier between them, sparkling small lights away from her across the ice of the river. She crept out into the darkness and saw fire poured out of the windows of her father's room. She screamed.

Down The Rabbit Hole

There were people close enough to hear the strangled cry that snapped out of her like a dropped glass. They put down their stolen things and approached.

If she hadn't been Alice In Wonderland and if she didn't have anything but magic to believe in and if she wasn't grown in an imagination of knowing anything can be, she wouldn't have been able to see the white rabbit pass in front of her again.

She ran after him, following him away, and she was into shadows that the mob couldn't see through.

The rabbit led her to a hole that went down safely into winter flowers and another world and what she felt was like falling asleep and dreaming.

9:45 PM
August 23, 1989

Chapter 66: An Opera At The End Of Its Time

They were sitting on the flat edge of the planet with their legs dangling over in the coolness of nothing. Where all Manifest Destinies ended and America with nothing left to conquer slipped off the edge and away, they were on the last standing rock and at their side a 1951 orchestra strung fishing lines of Opera out across the abyss. She wanted to show him this, where it all ended because she thought he'd be interested. America really was nothing more than just time and sand that filled an hourglass for a moment before. He watched all things of America pile over the edge, but was most affected by a thunderstorm with lightning of an August night he remembered fall away past him. He must have been just a teenager when that had happened long ago and he had watched it through his bedroom window, counting the space between flashes of lightning and the boom responses of thunder and he was glad to know that the seconds were getting longer and the storm was leaving. Seeing that moment disappear of all the moments of America, that was enough and he had seen enough, he didn't want to see anymore of America falling, and so she led him back to the roped balloon and they went the opposite way as America crashed off the edge behind them.

Page from original manuscript

Waking up...and dreaming.

9 781945 176609